BL.

CYBORG RANGER

CLARISSA LAKE

ISBN: 9798724995603

ASIN: B08VG278CW

WARNING: This book is an Erotic Sci-fi Romance with **multiple explicit sex scenes** and some mentions of rape. While it contains erotic sex scenes, it is not erotica. It also contains incidents of graphic violence. If these are triggers for you, please do not buy or read this book.

Clarissa Lake's Other Works:

Szeqart Prison Planet Series
Soliv Four

Narovian Mates Series
Dream Alien
Alien Alliances
Her Alien Captain
Her Alien Trader

Farseek Mercenary Series
Commander's Mate
Lieutenant's Mate
Sahvin's Mate
Argen's Mate
Faigon's Mate

Farseek Warrior Series
Kragyn
Narzek
Roran

Wicked Ways

Interstellar Matchmaking
Korjh's Bride
Rader's Bride
Joven's Bride

with Christine Myers
Jolt Somber
Talia's Cyborg
Axel Rex

Dagger Jack

Find all my books at:
https://amazon.com/author/clarissalake

Website: http://clarissalake.authors.zone/

Visit my website at and sign up for my newsletter.

Everyone who signs up will get a free ebook.

CONTENTS

ONE

Blaze Savage stood on the observation deck looking at the blue and white ball, in the distance, Earth home. He hadn't been back since his awakening over nine decades before. Barely a second passed and the burly cyborg accessed his central processor to recall the specific amount of time. He'd left Earth 97 years, 5 months, 18 days, 10 hours, 40 minutes, 25.7 seconds ago.

He had two reasons for coming back to Earth. After several years decompressing on Phantom, the cyborg planet, after the war, he wanted to put his talents to better use in Vyken Dark's new Cyborg Ranger project. The other reason was to find his genetic mate.

Blaze was returning to Earth with five other cyborgs, who had volunteered for the program. Even though the genetic mating project only about one in ten cyborgs had found the mates that were promised at the end of their service in the war. That was partly because only females in Enclave territories got tested.

Of millions of cyborgs on Phantom, few

had mates. Only a small percentage of the population were female. Most of them were mated female cyborgs.

When Commander Dark contacted him with plans to restore order west of the enclave territories, it sounded like Blaze's kind of job. Blaze and the other five were Cyborg Rangers who went on some of the most dangerous missions in the war. Dark thought this team would be better suited to the challenges of restoring civilization to the territories south and west of the Enclave and its Annex.

The Mesaarkans bombed the major cities on every continent, most of the towns and rural areas were untouched. Some were autonomous, while others were ruled by gangs and overlords. Those ruled by the overlords held their ordinary residents hostage in their own communities with gangers enforcing their whims. Farringay was off limits, but the west was open for restoration.

The Enclave decided to pull as much of that territory as possible into the fold. Vyken Dark could have sent any number of virtually trained, newly Awakened cyborgs. But their training was AI generated while they were in stasis. The Cyborg Rangers were real time, experienced combat specialists. They would do the recon before Vyken sent in the newbie protectors for the rangers to supervise. The territory would be divided among the six rangers.

Also, on the transport bringing them to Earth were a couple of lucky cyborgs who were genetically matched to women in the Enclave databank. All the cyborgs produced both at the Enclave and the Peruvian facility were maintained there. No additions to the civilian genetic databank had been added since the war.

The Rangers would add to that databank in their travels while newbie Dagger Jack was collecting data in the current Enclave territories. Somewhere in between, Blaze hoped he could find his mate. Meanwhile, he would have plenty to keep him busy.

Blaze watched Earth grow in his line of vision as they got closer to orbit. It was almost time for him to board the shuttle to New Chicago the only city restored in the territory. His duffle lay on the floor at his feet.

He picked it up and slung it over his shoulder as the order to go to the shuttle came through the internal cyborg network. Fifteen minutes later Blaze and his cohorts Shadow Hawk, Max Steel, Darken Wolf, Stalker Knight, and Falcon Rader were debarking from the shuttle and striding to the transport to the Enclave south of the city.

New Chicago was smaller than the original, reflecting the reduction in population of the entire world by the Mesaarkans' sneak attack just over a century before. The new city was ultra-modern comprised of gleaming sky scrapers and assorted smaller buildings with multiple green spaces.

The cyborgs had their own base near the underground facility which had been converted to residences and a small hospital. It was just a ten-minute flight from the space shuttle port in the low flying hover craft.

The six brawny cyborgs all over six feet tall made an impressive sight as they strode purposely toward the cyborg base with their duffels slung over their shoulders. They were all dressed identically in the black cargo pants and snug fitting khaki t-shirts. A few women working on the grounds paused to gaze at them, but the cyborg males barely noticed them.

It didn't matter how attractive the females were, they weren't mates for any of the cyborgs. The enhanced Cyborg Rangers were focused on their mission briefing with Commander Dark.

"Welcome back to Earth gentlemen. I know it wasn't what we were promised, but those who made those promises no longer exist," Vyken said when they were all seated around the table in the conference room. "We're the only ones left to clean up the remnants of civilization left after the initial attack by the Mesaarkans. We've done multiple fly overs for recon but we didn't want to send newbies to deal with frustrated naturals. You have the uploads of the maps we compiled of the most significant populated areas.

"Your primary job is to investigate and intervene where civilians are in danger from gangs or forced into human trafficking." Dark continued. "Once you've established the state of their communities, the Enclave will send representatives to invite them into the Enclave. We couldn't do anything about Farringay and Alexander Berke's holdings, but the Federation is giving us free rein on the western territories. Any questions?"

"Did your recon show any troublesome activity?" Blaze asked.

"The largest cities in your territory are in ruins and run by overlords with ganger enforcers. You won't be able to take them back on your own, so don't even try. The best thing we can do is evacuate the innocents that you find. Report back to us and we will send in teams and transport to move them to safe locations." Commander Dark replied. "Anyone else?" He paused for a few seconds then said, "Your hovercycles are waiting for you in the transport garage. While they are about as old as we are, they have all been refurbished with crystal drives and their nanite technology allows you to shift them into personal flyers. They are synchronized with your internal processor so no one else can operate them. Ping me any time if you need anything. You are all dismissed."

With that, all the cyborgs stood and headed out of the building to claim their assigned vehicles. Each cycle was numbered and they already knew which was theirs from the infodump they received when they volunteered for this assignment.

The sky cycles were strictly two person vehicles, that resembled old style water jet skis more than motorcycles, but longer. Behind the riders' seats was a compartment to carry their small duffels and spare weapons. There was also a sling on the right side for an ion rifle, and each cycle was loaded with one.

Blaze pulled his weapons belt from his duffle and strapped it on over his lean hips. It contained a blaster, half a dozen throwing knives and a large combat knife. He added a smaller laser pistol to his boot holster, then pulled on a black, synthetic leather jacket. While it looked, felt and smelled like real leather, it was man made.

Lastly, he pulled on his replica of an Australian bush hat that they had adopted as part of their Ranger regalia. The only indications of their authority were the Cyborg Ranger patches on the fronts of their jackets.

Blaze climbed on his sky cycle, started the motor and connected with the onboard AI to extend the wings and form the cockpit. He pulled slowly out of the garage and raised the craft vertically into the sky. When he reached the desired height then set off like a jet southward to his territory, formerly know as Texas.

The sun was shining in a cloudless blue sky. Below the Earth was verdant and green, and he found joy in racing across the sky in this fully refurbished multipurpose craft. Blaze hadn't been back to Earth since he shipped out to war barely a week after he was taken out of stasis.

He'd blamed the world for everything that happened to him in the war. The ninety-seven days in a Mesaarkan prison, the loss of his team. He'd been tortured repeatedly, injected with drugs, beaten, tormented with shock sticks to give them intel on the Federation. The irony was that Blaze didn't have the information to give. They wouldn't accept that he couldn't lie.

Vyken Dark and his team had gotten Blaze out of that prison and took out that whole Mesaarkan stronghold. He got three months to recover before they put him back out into the war. He fought one campaign after another on dozens of planets for the next sixty-five years.

They treated cyborgs like they were machines, granted, their emotions were dampened through programing and conditioning. Despite his enhancements Blaze was more human than machine. When Vyken Dark contacted him with this new job offer, he didn't hesitate.

Commander Dark pointed out that the people who made them and sent them to war were gone. Now was the time cyborgs could get the lives they were promised after the war,

a mate and a chance for a family. His life had
new purpose

TWO

Phoebe Brooks was hoeing out rows in her vegetable garden when she saw four men on horses galloping toward her homestead. Martin Stone's men. He called himself the Mayor of Grafton, but he was a gangster overlord who wanted her.

She dropped the hoe handle and pulled the ancient Glock from its holster to double check that it was fully loaded. She put it back in the holster and ran to her house where her shotgun was standing in the corner by the back door.

The riders hadn't reached her yard before she yanked open the back door and lunged inside. She didn't need to check that the long gun was loaded as she reloaded it every time, she shot it.

She took it up and marched out onto the back porch, pointed the gun at the four horsemen that reined their horses to the stop in her back yard. Phoebe didn't know all their names, but she recognized them as Martin Stone's thugs. Clade Joseph was the leader of this pack.

Phoebe thought maybe she should be honored that Stone thought enough of her to send his number one to relay whatever reason they'd ridden all the way from town to see her.

"Now, Phoebe, no need to shoot the messenger," Clade said. "Mr. Stone would like you to be his guest for dinner on Saturday. He asked me to deliver this note."

"It took four of you to deliver one note?" Phoebe blurted in a snarky tone. Her rifle aimed at Clade's chest.

Clade shrugged. "It's a long ride. One can't be too careful."

"Well, you can tell Stone I'm not going anywhere. It's planting season and I've got too much work to do to run around socializing. And who is going to watch the place so scavengers won't steal everything I've got?"

"He could send someone out to watch your place with the escort he sends to fetch you. You wouldn't need to do any of this if you'd just accept his proposal and come live in town." Clade reminded.

"Don't even start with that again. Just leave the note, and get off my land."

Clade urged his horse forward.

21

"Don't come any closer." Phoebe motioned with her shotgun. "Just drop it, and I will pick it up after you leave."

"I need an answer before I leave."

"You got my answer. I'm not coming to dinner. I don't want to see Stone, and I don't want to marry him."

"I don't know what he said in his note. But maybe if you read it, you'll change your mind." Clade held it up.

"Fine, drop it on the ground and I will pick it up after you leave. You already have my answer. I'm not going to dinner Saturday or any other time," she repeated.

"Well, ma'am, Mr. Stone can be just as stubborn as you. If you won't come to him, he will come to you."

"And he won't be any more welcome than you. The answer is no. I just want to be left alone."

Clade tossed the paper note through the air toward Phoebe, then turned his horse around and rode back the way he'd come with his three sidekicks. Only when they were tiny on the horizon did she lower her shotgun and go to pick up the piece of paper from the grass.

Holding her shotgun under her arm, pointed at the ground, she unfolded it and read the neatly hand printed message:

"Dearest Phoebe,

I know we've had our differences, but it has never changed the way I feel about you. It worries me greatly to think of you alone out on your ranch so far from town. I want to take care of you and protect you.

Won't you please grant me the honor of your company for dinner on Saturday so that we can discuss our future."

Warmest regards,

Martin"

Phoebe closed her eyes and shook her head. "Give it up, Martin. You don't want a wife you want an obedient submissive to play your sadistic sex games."

She crumpled the letter and stalked back into her house with it squeezed in a ball. After she, returned the shotgun to the corner by the door, she opened the door of her wood cookstove and tossed the wadded note into the embers and closed the door. Even as it caught fire, she knew this wouldn't be the end of it. When sweet sincerity didn't work, he would use force.

Clade and company would be back to grab her for Martin. Then she would be his prisoner. She hated to leave the home that had been in her family since before the Mesaarkan War. Its remote location is what saved it and the town of Graffton, population 6343. Not a high enough body count to rate one of their bombs left the town unscathed.

Phoebe couldn't see any other way out; she had to get away. She blinked as tears welled in her eyes. She'd made a good life for herself here with her goats and chickens, her garden and her big fluffy dog Brandi. Her dog would come with her, but she had no choice but to leave the other animals to fend for themselves. Her horse Sherry was the only transportation she had. That would limit what she could carry.

She would have to live off the land for the most part, but that didn't worry her. Leaving her homestead unguarded was risking to lose it. When Martin learned she was gone, he would probably destroy it. He didn't take rejection well, especially since she had fallen for his charming facade once. He didn't love her; he just wanted to own her and use her to satisfy his perversions.

Phoebe was open minded about sex, but Martin took dominance and submission to a torturous level. He had a secret room full of devices he used for sexual torture to punish her when she displeased him. The last time was the worst. She finally escaped. Ever since, she had been wary of anyone who approached her isolated homestead.

The few who stopped in passing were harmless. But she no longer trusted anyone. She met them all at gunpoint. Martin had a whole gang of thugs, and she knew she couldn't fight them all with a shotgun and a Glock. They could even come back today, once they told Martin how she'd greeted them.

What if they didn't go all the way back to town? Maybe they just rode away to make her drop her guard, and they would be back to take her by force. She couldn't rule that out. It was almost midday and she didn't have much time. She went to the linen closet and pulled out two of her sturdiest pillow cases and She packed three changes of clothes, soap, a small face cloth, and towel.

She found an old sleeping bag rolled up on a shelf in the back of her bedroom closet. Taking up the sleeping bag and pillow cases, she raced to the kitchen pantry and packed as much dried vegetables, dry beans and fruit as she could carry. Rummaging in the kitchen cupboards, she found an old mess kit for cooking and a canteen for water.

Phoebe didn't stop to check if everything was contained within. She couldn't shake the urgency to get away before Stone's men came back. At the back door, she added a small fishing kit, her hunting knife and all her spare ammo for her guns were the last things she added.

Tying the two pillow cases together to serve as saddle bags. Everything seemed to take so long, and she berated herself for not preparing in case she had to run. Martin had left her alone for the whole winter. Phoebe had begun to relax, thinking he'd accepted the fact that she didn't want to be with him.

It wasn't like he couldn't find someone else. Martin was handsome and powerful. He could be very charming when he was trying to get laid. He lost his charm when he showed his other side in his secret room.

Phoebe shuddered involuntarily at the memory. She had never screamed so much in her life, and it wasn't from pleasure. She vowed never to let him touch her again. She didn't want to see him or even think about him.

She managed to grab her jacket and

shotgun, carrying everything to the barn in one trip. Her mare Sherry came into the barn expecting her grain ration. Phoebe poured a scoop into the bucket hanging on the side of the stall. Sherry stood contentedly munching on the grain while Phoebe put on her saddle blanket, smoothed it out and added the saddle followed by her supplies and her shotgun.

Phoebe never went anywhere unarmed, even before the threat of Martin trying to charm his way back into her life. No amount of charm would make her forget that horrendous three days he had punished her for merely speaking to one of his men.

Sherry had finished her grain by the time she was ready to take off the halter and bridle the horse. Finally ready, Phoebe led the horse from the barn. She was about to mount, when she remembered the goats and the chickens. She ran to the pasture, opened the gate and then to the chicken pen.

They would probably all be gone if she ever came back but she couldn't let Martin or his men catch her. She couldn't worry about them; she had to get away.

Phoebe mounted the horse and urged her into a canter heading east, away from Grafton and away from Martin.

THREE

Blaze spent the first few days flying over old Texas, exploring the territory. The cities were in ruins as he'd expected, with smaller communities, farms, and ranches scattered in between the cities. There was activity around the farms and ranches but greatly reduced compared to the pre-war archives.

With the loss of the power grid, farm machinery couldn't be recharged. Not everyone had wind and solar generators. Those were clearly marked with disabled farm machinery sitting idle in the middle of fields with tall grass and weeds around them. Without the use of their automated systems, farms and ranches were forced to used methods such as those used in the late 19th and early 20th century.

Horses were again used as a mode of transportation. In just the few days he'd been patrolling his territory, Blaze had seen many horses used for travel. He'd been fully briefed on the state of the old USA. It would surely take more than a few cyborg rangers to bring order back in the territories between the pockets of civilization.

He was flying over east Texas heading for the Dallas ruins when he saw a lone horse and rider being chased down a rural road by a group of riders.

Blaze slowed his hover cycle and retracted the wing as he took the craft just above ground level and flew the cycle near enough to the loan rider to see she was female. He brought the cycle to a halt and pivoted in midair to face the five male riders chasing her.

Pulling out his ion rifle he raised the butt to his shoulder and aimed it at the male riders approaching. "Stop right there, gentlemen."

The men pulled up their horses about fifty feet from where Blaze hovered his cycle.

"Who the hell are you?" demanded the apparent leader.

"Captain Blaze Savage, Federation Cyborg Rangers. What did the female do to make the five of you race after her?"

"Well, I don't think that's any of your business," said the man who seemed to be in charge. He was the best dressed and sat on a superior horse."

"If she has committed a crime, it is my

business. If you are harassing her and attempting to deprive her of her freedom, that is also my business."

"My name is Martin Stone. I am the Mayor of Grafton. The woman is Phoebe Brooks, my girlfriend. We had a misunderstanding, and I am trying to catch up to her so we can work it out," he said smoothly.

But his accelerated heart rate told Blaze he was lying about something. "The fact that she was running makes me think she doesn't want to see you." With his enhanced vision, he could see that the horse was running full out. Whatever happened between her and the man in front of him was more than a misunderstanding. It looked more like she was running for her life.

"I just want to talk to her," Stone insisted.

That didn't ring true either. "I don't think she wants to hear you right now. It shouldn't take five men to get a lone woman to stop and listen. I think I need to hear her side of this story." Blaze hadn't lowered his rifle as he spoke to them. "Until I do, I am ordering you to stand down and go back to your town."

"As you pointed out there are five of us, and one of you," Stone said in a thinly veiled threat. As if on cue, the four men flanking him pulled out semi-automatic pistols and pointed them at Blaze.

He almost laughed. One sweep of his ion rifle and they would all be dead. He didn't even need the rifle. The bullets from their guns would hurt, even make him bleed but his nanites would quickly repair the damage. He had faced far worse in the war… And lived to file report on it.

"You do know; I'm a cyborg? I can drop you all with this ion rifle before you can fire a shot. You look doubtful. Do you want to try me?"

"Fuck this!" Martin Stone growled. "Let's go." He turned his horse back the way they had come, and holstering their guns his men turned their horses and followed him.

When Blaze was satisfied, they would keep going, he returned his ion rifle to its holster and turned his hover cycle around to follow Phoebe Brooks. He hovered over the crumbling pavement at the modest speed of 85mph.

He caught up to her within a few minutes, though she had gotten farther than he expected. Slowing his cycle well before he reached her, he glided along beside her. Although his vehicle was almost silent running at that slow speed, the horse shied and reared.

Phoebe tried valiantly to maintain her seat, but gravity was stronger.

Blaze stopped the cycle and leapt to catch her before she hit the ground. He couldn't get his balance in time to grasp her and remain standing. He could only cushion her fall as she landed on top of him.

They lay together on the highway stunned for a minute. Blaze was even more stunned as he inhaled her heady, delightful scent, and his cock twitched. It took him several seconds to make himself form words, while his mind filled with one single word: *Mine.*

"Are---are you, all right?" he asked.

"Thanks to you, but your machine made my horse shy and throw me in the first place."

"I know, I didn't expect that." Blaze sat up with Phoebe on his lap and gazed at her with such intensity that she averted her eyes. Then she struggled to get up, and he gripped her waist to help and rose to his feet as well."

"What made you follow me?" she asked, gazing up at him.

Well over six feet, the top of her head was

almost even with his shoulder. Blaze had no trouble understanding why Martin Stone wanted her. She was exquisite with expressive brown eyes and long dark hair tied back at the nape of her neck. Her curvy figure was just shy of voluptuous. Her mouth was full and looked soft and kissable.

He was so taken by her beauty that he didn't answer right away. "Those men following you. I stopped them to see why they were chasing you. The man Martin Stone claimed it was a misunderstanding."

"Oh, that bastard! There is no misunderstanding. He can't take no for an answer. I'll kill him if he comes near me," she vowed. "But, why did you get in the middle of this?"

"I'm a Federation Cyborg Ranger, assigned to uphold the laws that once governed this territory. The name is Blaze Savage."

"What's a cyborg?"

"A genetically enhanced human with an onboard computer interface in my brain. We were created to fight the war," he explained, not taking his eyes from her face.

"You mean like a superhero?"

"More like a super soldier... stronger,

33

faster, more resilient than natural born humans," he said. "But, tell me more about the circumstances with Stone."

"He's an abusive, sadistic pervert. He held me prisoner in his own personal torture chamber. I got away, but not before he put me through three days of pure hell."

Blaze's eyes flashed a look of murderous rage. "He hurt you?" *He's a dead man walking.*

Phoebe nodded solemnly. "That was last fall. He stayed away all winter, then he sent his men with a charming little invitation for dinner to discuss our future a week ago. I packed up and abandoned my home as soon as they were out of sight. They almost caught me... If you hadn't stopped them..."

She shuddered with the nightmare memories of her last encounter with Martin Stone. She would have said more, but her throat tightened as angry tears threatened.

Blaze finally gave in to the temptation, stepping close and wrapping her in his arms. Holding her was the most wonderful thing he'd ever felt. The wave of emotion that engulfed him was almost overwhelming.

FOUR

Phoebe had heard the riders coming as she'd just saddled her horse. Her dog Brandy had gone off exploring but a sharp whistle would bring her running. The sound of multiple horses was getting louder too fast. She was out of time; she could only leave her sleeping bag and supplies behind.

Mounting her horse quickly, she cried, "run Sherry!" and kicked her in the sides. The horse responded without balking and lunged forward into a gallop. In another universe, she could have been a race horse because she loved to run, and she was fast.

Sherry ran full out with Phoebe urging her with her voice and her hands. She never used spurs or riding crops. As fast as the horse could run, it wasn't fast enough. Glancing behind, Phoebe saw the four riders were gradually catching up. Her horse had already sprinted over a mile at full gallop. The mare was starting to tire, but she kept her pace as though she sensed the urgency of her rider to flee.

The next time Phoebe looked behind her, the riders had stopped. She didn't know why, but she wasn't waiting around to find out. However, she did slow the horse to a canter, thinking she might circle back to get the rest of her supplies if they really had stopped chasing her. They continued at an easy canter for several minutes and slowed to a trot.

Phoebe knew her mare would run her heart out if she asked it. She wouldn't ask it. The horse was a companion animal almost as much as her dog. Thinking of the dog, Brandy never liked Martin. Even when he tried to make friends with her, the dog shied away from him and growled. That should have been her first clue.

As she contemplated slowing Sherry to a walk, hoping the dog would catch up with them, a vehicle seemed to materialize beside them. It startled both Phoebe and the horse, making the animal shy and rear. She couldn't hold on and she was falling.

For a moment, she seemed to be suspended in midair, waiting for her body to slam down onto the pavement. Only, that didn't happen. Her fall was instead cushioned by a firm male body.

After he helped her up and stood up, so she got a good look at him, she felt a shock of attraction. She tried to shake it off as she told him about the men who were chasing her. That last man she'd let into her life half killed her before she escaped.

Phoebe thought she was strong, and she could usually take care of herself. Martin Stone had made her doubt it, and her own judgement for letting him into her life.

She was so enraged at Martin and herself, it was all she could do to stop the angry tears that threatened. Then the big cyborg ranger took her into his arms and held her against his chest. Her first instinct was to pull away, but right then his solid chest and his strong arms around her felt too damn good.

She laid her head against his chest and breathed in his scent of lavender soap and male, sliding her arms around his waist. It felt good to lean on someone bigger and stronger, just for a little while. Except, then she felt his arousal against her belly.

He was male. What did she expect? She didn't expect her nipples to tighten and the clenching between her thighs. She drew back a little to look up at his face. He gave her a wry grin.

Phoebe felt her face heat. He knew she was aroused. She started to look away, but he put his fingers under her chin and coaxed her to look up at him again.

"There is no shame in desiring your male---the one genetic mate who is meant only to be *yours*."

"What? What are you saying?"

"You are my genetic mate."

"How do you know?

"Pheromones. Your scent arouses me."

Phoebe put her hands against his chest and pushed away from him. He seemed to understand that she needed the space.

"That's why you are attracted to me."

"And you know this because…?" She gave him a skeptical look.

"I scent your arousal."

She opened her mouth to give him a snappy reply but he was right. She wanted him. It was way too easy to think about getting naked with him with that hard, sexy body against her. The bulge she felt against her lower abdomen seemed ample to satisfy her.

"Do you want to breed?" he asked like he was asking if she wanted honey in her tea.

He was dead serious.

"Um, not right now. I think I would like to get to know you a little better."

"What would you like to know?" he asked.

Before she could answer the familiar bark of her dog drew her attention. The dog ran toward her, wagging its tail. Brandy surprised her by going to sniff Blaze. The big collie shepherd wagged her tail and stood on her hind legs with her paws against his middle.

"Wow, I've never seen her do that before. She likes you." Phoebe looked at him thoughtfully.

"Do you?" he asked bluntly.

She shrugged. "I think I'd like to find out."

By then, Sherry had gotten over her fright and came walking up to Phoebe and the ranger. The horse stopped to check Phoebe nudging her gently and nickering to her. Then she turned to Blaze, stretching her neck to sniff him. She nickered again and nodded her head.

"I guess she likes you, too."

Blaze just smiled at Phoebe, like he was just as pleased to be in her company as they were. "Where will you go?"

"First, I need to go back to my camp and get my supplies. Those men were too close, they would have caught me."

"Do you not have a home?"

"I do, but I couldn't stay there. They would have just kidnapped me," she said. "Martin Stone thinks he is the law around here, and his thugs are his enforcers."

"He is an overlord and they are his gangers."

Blaze stepped close to her again; so close, she could feel his body heat. Phoebe could only stare up at him, mesmerized as he framed her face his in hands. "I just have to kiss you."

Her lips parted; and she forgot to breathe as he lowered his mouth to hers. His kiss was tender, at first, as his tongue slipped between her parted lips to caress the inside of her mouth. She made kitten sounds in her throat as she pressed her body to his, unable to resist.

Phoebe wound her arms around his neck and crushed her breasts against his chest to ease the ache in her nipples. Heat pooled between her thighs as sensations of raw need surged through her body to her clit, making her core clench on itself.

Blaze wrapped her in his arms lifting her off the ground so they were chest to chest. One of his hands cupped her ass and pressed her firmly so his hard cock was against her core.

It was a good thing he hadn't done this before he asked if she wanted to breed with him. With her whole body clamoring for exactly that, she knew that she did. She might have said the words out loud had her mouth not been fused to his and her tongue getting intimately acquainted with his.

But they couldn't just get naked in the middle of the road and fuck while his hover cycled idled and her horse and dog stood by. That would be crazy! It would also leave them vulnerable.

That little voice of reason in her head made her pull back from his mind-numbing kiss even though she could sense his reluctance.

His eyes were dark with a possessive glint. The way he was looking at her made her want to be his and everything else that it meant. Even so, she also knew that she wasn't ready for breeding just yet.

Blaze let her slide down his front until her feet were on the ground again. He brought up one hand, stroking her cheek with his fingers pushing a stray lock of hair back from her face. Phoebe stared up at his face. He was gorgeous, and he was looking at her like she was his dream come true.

"We should go back to your camp and collect your supplies," he said. "Then we will go to your home."

"It will take days to get back to my homestead with my horse. I've been traveling for almost a week. They never went back to town after I ran them off. There's no other way they could have caught up to me. Martin was wise not to show his face when he sent his lackeys to give me that sweet little note. I would have shot him."

"How far is your homestead from here?"

"Maybe seventy miles. I didn't want to push Sherry that hard, and I rode on the pavement so we wouldn't be so easy to track."

"I will request a transport for your animals. My sky cycle can only transport two people and limited essentials."

"I can't just leave them here, though."

FIVE

"I'll put a tracker on your horse's bridle. I want to do a fly over to see if those males are heading back the way they came. Will you come with me? I don't want to leave you here alone." Blaze gripped her upper arms gently."

"And we will come back for Sherry and Brandy?"

"Yes." He nodded.

"Could we go as far as my homestead and still find them when we come back? I left my livestock to fend for themselves."

Blaze released her and walked over to his cycle and opened a compartment under the seat. Plucking out a tiny round disk between his thumb and forefinger, he walked over to the horse. Reaching for her bridal slowly so she wouldn't shy, he pressed the disc to her bridle. With that done, he went back and climbed onto the cycle, then held out his hand to Phoebe.

She gave him a slight nod and put her hand in his, climbing on behind him.

"Put your arms around me and hold on."

As she did so, Blaze sent the sky/hover cycle into the air back the way they came. He guided it just above the tree tops so he could see the road farther ahead than if he hovered just above the pavement.

He smiled to himself that Phoebe held him more tightly than he thought possible. Her breasts were squeezed against his back and her cheek pressed just below the base of his neck. His female---Phoebe was *his* female.

The thought looped in the back of his mind while he turned his attention to the road ahead. Only minutes passed before he caught sight of the five horsemen who'd been trying to chase Phoebe down. She was probably right that they'd been trailing her for days.

The five of them looked up as they noticed the shadow of his vehicle pass over them. Blaze extended the wings and gunned the propulsion system, climbing higher speeding back down the road toward where he calculated Phoebe's homestead would be if she had traveled as far as she thought.

His heart sank for her when he found the place, he thought was hers. Only a small barn stood, and what might have been a house was a pile of smoldering rubble. There were dead animals lying near the barn and chicken pen.

He glided around the destruction and turned the cycle facing away from it.

He drew in a breath and let it out, wishing he didn't have to tell her, but knowing it would hurt her even more to surprise her with it. "I believe I have found your homestead."

"Oh good. Can we land?"

"Yes, but it's not good. The house is burned and there are dead animals."

"No! Oh, no!" she cried in disbelief. "That bastard!"

Blaze just nodded, lowering the cycle to the ground facing away from the devastated scene. Anger was what she needed to get through this. One way or another, he would end Martin Stone's reign over this territory. Just killing him was too kind. He needed to suffer, to lose his power and his possessions, then maybe be marooned naked in the desert with no water.

Phoebe climbed off first but didn't turn around before Blaze got off. She stood with her fists clenched at her sides with her eyes closed steeling herself to see the scene he'd described. Slowly she turned and opened them.

The house was burnt to the ground with what was left of the roof's center peak resting on the foundation. "Damn you!" she screamed, drawling the 'you' out into a sob. "Damn you, Martin."

Blaze wanted to hold her and comfort her, but he didn't know how he could make this better. His female had been deeply wronged. Martin Stone was not a man in love as he claimed. He was an evil man bent on revenge on a woman who had rejected him.

Phoebe marched toward the barn, crying softly and he grimaced, following her. Six little goat bodies were strewn over the grass including two babies. All of them shot with a projectile weapon.

The flies buzzing over them and the mutilated carcasses indicated they had been dead for days. Several hens and parts lay dead outside the chicken pen, apparently shot as well.

Phoebe covered her mouth and choked back a sob. In that quiet moment, the sounds of cheeping came from inside the hen house. Then a plump brown hen stood in the doorway clucking. "Oh, my God!" she exclaimed softly. "They must have missed you because you were sitting on eggs and now you have babies."

Momentarily, they heard the bleat of a

goat, then a second one. One lone mama goat and her baby came trotting around the barn, apparently lured by the sound Phoebe's familiar voice. "The bastards didn't get them all."

Blaze stood watching and waiting, feeling pride in the strength he saw in his female. On the brink of despair, she had become defiant as she found some of her stock alive.

She turned back to look at her ruined home. "This house has been in my family since before the war. All the things passed down through generations were in there, and he ruined it for me. How could he even think I would go back to him after what he did? Could he actually believe that if I lost everything, I would come back to him?"

"He's not too smart if he did, my female," Blaze said softly.

"Oh, I know why he did it. He wanted to hurt me as if he hadn't done enough of that already. I pity the people in Grafton with him running it."

He went to her side and put his arm around her shoulders. "He won't be running it much longer. The people of this territory are now protected under laws of the Civil Restoration

Enclave of North America. They are expanding their territory to get rid of ruling tyrants like Martin Stone."

"I am so angry that he did this! I wish I had laid in wait for him and shot him on sight. Instead, I ran like a coward."

"No, there were five of them, and the range of your weapons is limited. Sometimes, it's smarter to retreat and wait for a better circumstance to eliminate your enemy."

"I want to help you take him down. I raised that herd from babies. Slaughtering them like that was about the meanest thing they could have done. We had cattle when I was a kid, but goats were easier to manage alone."

"How long have you been here alone?" Blaze asked.

"Five years since my Mom died. She wasn't even that old. She got sick one year and six months later she died. There was nothing we could do. The medicine woman could only ease her pain with herbal remedies."

"Will you come stay at my cabin? Your home is gone and it's not safe for you to stay here alone."

"Convenient for you," she said with a sidelong glance at him.

It took him a moment to get that she was teasing him.

"What about them?"

"I have requested transport."

"When did you do that? How did you do that?"

"My integrated computer, on the cyborg network. They should arrive in an hour and ten minutes."

"Well, I can see there is a lot more to you than just good looks," she said and smiled at him. "Tell me something."

"What?"

"When you kissed me back there... My mouth felt kind of tickly afterward. What was that? Should I be worried?" She turned toward him, his arm remaining about her shoulders.

"It was nanocybots migrating into your mouth. They are submicroscopic robots that heal me when I am injured. As you get more of them, they will heal you as well and prevent illnesses."

"My mom could have used some of them."

"Our medics now used them to help unenhanced humans recover from injuries and illnesses." Blaze turned and pulled Phoebe against him with both arms around her. He just couldn't get enough of looking at her. The emotions that flooded through him were nearly staggering.

His whole life had been about his duty to fight for the Federation, his obligation to risk his life to protect ordinary humans, like the ones who started the bloody war over territory. The natural humans were bigoted against the genetically engineered and cybernetically enhanced cyborgs. They called them machines, treated them like they had no emotions and no rights except to serve the Federation.

Many were horribly injured in the early years of the war and left to die alone in battlefields on distant planets because they were considered expendable. Blaze had been one of them.

He told Phoebe his story while they found a crate for the hen and her babies to move them when the transport arrived. She also found a rope to tether her pigmy nanny goat and her kid.

SIX

Too weak to fight, the Mesaarkans captured him and kept him weakened with drugs and torture. Ninety-seven days of torment, now archived in his memory banks. Finally, Vyken Dark and his combat team rescued him.

The single thing that kept him sane was the promise etched into his genes that one day he would have this moment. He would find the one female who was his genetic complement.

It was surreal that she was now in his arms and he was looking down into her eyes. He was almost euphoric with the joy of finding her, enraged at the same time at the damage Martin Stone had done to her.

Blaze was glad Commander Dark had called him to come back to take this job. It could have been months, even years before he found his female. He was mentally prepared for that, but it only took weeks.

He would have protected any female in Phoebe's predicament, but he wouldn't be attracted to just any female. Only Phoebe. He knew the moment she landed on top of him in the middle of that road.

Dark had warned him that it wasn't the same for the females. They didn't always trust the attraction they felt for their cyborgs in the beginning. Cyborgs were engineered so that they loved an avatar of their female all their lives, and that love transferred to their genetic mate.

Phoebe's breath caught as she looked up at his face. He seemed utterly smitten, and that tender look was for *her*. It seemed like he really wanted to kiss her but hesitated, like maybe he was waiting for a sign from her that she wanted to be kissed.

She ran her hands up over his muscular chest and put her arms around his neck. Raising herself on her toes she pressed her lips to his lightly. He was all male and gorgeous, and he'd said he was hers. That, and he smelled so good.

The sweet gesture was all the invitation Blaze needed to deepen the kiss. His tongue swirled around hers as he cupped her buttocks and lifted her so her mons pressed against his erection. Phoebe lifted her legs, wrapping them loosely around his narrow hips. All that sensual input surged to her clit and she moaned into his mouth.

By the time Blaze ended the kiss, they were both trembling with desire. "I want you so much," he growled. "But I don't want our first time to be at the ruins of your home."

"I appreciate that," she drew in a shaky breath, caressing his cheek with her fingers. "I knew about the war, but I never knew they made men like you to fight it."

"There were a million of us. The first attack of the Mesaarkans destroyed Earth's communication network and killed millions of people. The Federation was fully extended fighting them all over space. There weren't resources to restore mass communications on Earth."

"How long did you fight in the war?"

"Ninety-five years, five months, and 22 days."

"You… You're over a hundred years old?" She was stunned. "You hardly look thirty-five."

"Ninety-eight. They accelerate growth so cyborgs matured in just a year. I spent three years on the cyborg colony Phantom."

Phoebe ran her fingers through the hair on the back of his head beneath the worn bush hat he wore. She was contemplating another delectable kiss on his full male lips when a faint whine caught their attention.

"That's our transport," Blaze said, letting her down to stand on the ground. It stopped in midair and settled in the barnyard outside the fence.

Phoebe watched in awe. It was the biggest vehicle she had ever seen. "That certainly looks big enough to carry a horse... Several horses."

A door in the side opened and a tall male with red hair stepped out. "Captain Savage," he greeted with a nod of respect. "Javen Black. I brought the livestock transport since you are transporting a horse."

"Thank you. We must pick up the horse about seventy miles from here. I put a tracker on it, so we should be able to find it easily," Blaze replied.

"We just have some chickens and two little goats here. The bastards who burned my house killed the rest."

"And they will pay for it," Blaze asserted.

"You must be the Captain's female." Javen dipped his head. No introduction was necessary. Blaze already reported finding her to headquarters.

"I will get the chickens. Can you get the goats?" he asked her.

"Of course, I can carry the baby and she will follow."

After the animals were loaded, Blaze pinged the tracker on the horse and gave Javen the coordinates. "We will meet you there. We need to make a quick stop to pick up Phoebe's belongings from her camp."

The transport lifted off while Blaze and Phoebe walked back by the burnt ruins of her house to get on his cycle. She cast a last rueful glance at it, then climbed on behind her cyborg.

He raised the cycle into the air and transformed it into a sky cycle. It shot forward as though it were rocket propelled and they reached the point where Blaze calculated her camp was. He receded the cover and glided around the area until they spotted it.

Thankfully Stone and his men hadn't found

the camp. The possessions in her makeshift pack were all she had left. Blaze helped her gather them up and secure them on the cycle. They reached the meeting point within minutes of the transport landing.

Phoebe put two fingers into her mouth and gave a loud whistle. Within seconds, Brandy and Sherry came trotting toward them. The mare, Sherry balked at entering the stock compartment in the back until she heard the nannie goat bleat.

Although she wanted to ride to the cabin with Blaze, they agreed that her riding with the horse in the transport would help keep her calm. As the ramp that also served as the back door closed Phoebe was still a little stunned by the abrupt course change of her life. She hoped it would be a good one.

SEVEN

Blaze's cabin was remotely located in northeast Texas, probably an abandoned vacation home from an earlier era. It was only half the size of Phoebe's house, with a small shed just big enough for her horse. A large yard had been cut out of wooded grassland, now overgrown in tall grass and saplings. The transport crushed a stand of them when it settled to the ground. That was her view when the rear door of the vehicle opened.

There was no fenced area to contain the animals and no separate containment for the hen and her babies. It was early spring, so the climate was mild enough for the animals to be outside until they could arrange something better.

Blaze was there to meet them already; his sky cycle was capable of speeds beyond the cumbersome stock transport. Brandy trotted out the opening and huffed a greeting to Blaze, wagging her tail.

"I know this isn't as nice as your barn for the animals, but I have a plan," Blaze assured her with a wide welcoming smile.

Phoebe opened the stall and led her saddled horse down the ramp. When they were on the ground, Blaze went up the ramp to get the chicken crate and release the tiny goats.

Meanwhile, Javen opened the side door and ramp. A bot-tram rolled down the ramp loaded with sections of interlocking fence panels made from a lightweight material. Phoebe recognized it as such immediately when it came into view. She was surprised that he thought of it.

The bot-tram rolled across the yard and stopped beside the shed, unloading the panels into a pile. Javen closed the stock ramp while waiting for the bot-tram to drop its load and return to the transport. A second bot brought two bags of feed, depositing them inside the shed.

"Thanks for getting this together on short notice, Javen. I appreciate it," Blaze said to the younger cyborg.

"I am honored, sir," he dipped his head briefly then returned to the transport.

Phoebe hadn't missed the deference the transport pilot gave her cyborg. Yes, she had already begun to think of him as hers. Just the memory of the passionate kisses in his arms back at her homestead caused a flutter between her thighs.

She shook herself mentally and led her horse toward the shed as Blaze opened it. The mare was probably more than ready to have the saddle removed. The building was bigger than it looked when she got the mare inside. There was room for a horse stall, a smaller one for the goats, and the chicken crate. It even had an old wooden sawhorse she could use as a saddle stand.

Phoebe unsaddled the horse while Blaze brought in two fence panels to make the stall and fastened them to the wall. They snapped together in the front corner and were just flexible enough to bend open to get the horse in and out. He pulled the front panel open just enough to let Phoebe out.

"We'll close them inside while we set up the fence," he said.

Outside, Phoebe paused to look around. The yard was about two acres cut out of thick woods on all four sides. "Where are we? From where I lived?" she clarified.

"Three hundred twenty-seven-point-two miles northeast. You are safe here, Phoebe," he assured her. "Without tech, Martin Stone would never find this place."

"Good."

"But, don't worry, I will take care of him," he said. "Right now, I need to get your animals contained and bond with you, my female."

He met her gaze with a heated look that left little doubt about what he had in mind. Her body reacted again with desire making it hard to concentrate.

The pile of fencing had doubled in size when she emerged from the shed. "How did it get so big?"

"It was compressed. This should be enough to cover half the area of this clearing."

Phoebe nodded. "That should be enough pasture to start."

"And we can change the shape any time we want," he said, lifting a panel and handing it to her. He took another section, carried it to the other side of the shed, and used a tool unfamiliar to Phoebe to fasten it perpendicular to the shed's corner. He motioned to her to bring her section, showing her how to connect it to the first.

Each section's vertical supports had spikes that extended into the dirt to hold it in place.

Blaze had already calculated the number of square feet of that single bundle of fence panels. Working together, they completed the task in just about an hour. The horse and the little goats were then released into the newly enclosed pasture.

By the time they finished, Blaze had realized Phoebe was swaying on her feet with exhaustion. It occurred to him that she likely hadn't eaten all day and probably hadn't gotten enough sleep the several nights she'd spent on the run.

Much as he wanted to breed with her and make her his mate, she looked too tired to enjoy it. He told himself he could wait even though his cock seemed to rebel.

"Let's go inside and get something to eat," he said.

She nodded and gave him a faint smile. She looked so tired that he scooped her up in his arms and carried her into the cabin. She just laid her head on his shoulder and let him.

The living area was contained in one room.

61

They entered through the kitchen, which included a small table for two mounted on the corner wall. The chairs were hardwood, so Blaze passed them for the softer sofa and deposited her there.

"I'll get you a meal bar and some fruit juice. I'm afraid I don't have much variety of food."

"That's okay, I'm not fussy. I've been eating jerky and dried vegetables. I don't even feel that hungry, but I know I should eat. It's been a rough few days." She leaned her head back on the sofa and closed her eyes.

Blaze was back in only a couple minutes, but Phoebe had dozed off in that time. He set the food and juice on the table and sat beside her. Putting his arm around her shoulders, he gave her a little shake and said her name.

She opened her eyes, looking a little disoriented for a moment, then smiled at him and took the glass of juice he offered. She drank half of it in several gulps. It had been hours since she'd had anything to drink.

Blaze handed her the meal bar with the wrapper peeled back, and opened one for himself. By the time they both finished eating mildly flavored bars and drank their juice,

Phoebe seemed to perk up. She got up and asked for the bathroom, and he pointed the way.

When she came back, he held out his hand to her, pulled her down onto his lap when she took it. He cupped her cheek with his hand and used his thumb to tilt her face back for a kiss.

The first kiss was a soft caress to her lips, then he ran the tip of his tongue over them. She opened her mouth to tease him with her tongue. It was all the invitation he needed to fuse his mouth to hers in a deep passionate kiss.

As it went on, Phoebe turned and straddled his lap, pressing her chest to his, with her mons pressed against his erection. Nothing had ever felt so good as having his female in his arms. He was elated by the passion in her response.

She put her arms around his neck and caressed his head as they kissed again and again. Phoebe was as aroused as he; her scent filled his nostrils. Unable to wait, he stood with her wrapped around him and carried her to the far end of the cabin.

He stood her beside his bed and framed her face in his hands, staring at her in wonder. The years of war that haunted him, driving him to a life of solitude on Phantom, faded into the backfiles of his CPU. This was a whole new phase in his life.

"You are so beautiful, Phoebe. Tell me you want to breed with me…" he whispered.

She opened her mouth to speak, but no sound came out. Grasping his hands, she turned her face to kiss one palm and then the other, met his gaze, and nodded.

Things were happening fast, but the men in her life had been few and far between. She had never been this attracted and this aroused by any of them.   She wanted Blaze. It was as simple as that.   How he treated her afterward would determine where things went from there.

EIGHT

"I wish to... breed? ...With you," she whispered back, meeting his gaze. "If you mean sex, I'd be lying if I said no. I can't deny what I felt in your arms. It scares me a little."

"You never have to fear me. It was the promise of you that kept me alive all the years I spent fighting the war." Blaze said the words with such reverence that she could only believe him.

She nodded, never taking her eyes from his face.

Phoebe was nervous about the moment before it came. The memory of what Martin Stone did to her still left her shaken, but the caring she saw in Blaze's eyes was as arousing as his magnificent physique.

Blaze pulled his khaki green t-shirt untucked from his black cargo pants, pulling it off over his head. She stared for a moment at his broad, muscular chest, then reached down and pulled her worn t-shirt over her head.

Her ample breasts were crisscrossed with a length of fabric tied in the front that supported them. As she untied it, Blaze flicked his gaze from her eyes to her chest, watching with great interest as she unbound them. Her nipples had tightened into erect tips, and her pussy fluttered.

Looking at the prominent bulge in his pants, then up at his face, she untied the belt on her old worn jeans, toeing off a battered pair of sneakers, and pushed the jeans down over the curves of her hips. The catch and the zipper hadn't worked since she found them in an old plastic box in the attic.

Phoebe straightened, took a deep breath, put her shoulders back, and looked up at him in all her naked glory. She'd wanted him since the first time he'd kissed her, as though her body knew he was meant to be hers. She was going to have what she wanted. Pleasure had been all too scarce in her life for the last few years.

She looked meaningfully at his pants, then up at his face. Blaze smiled, daring her to make the next move. So, she stepped closer, slid her fingers underneath the waist of his cargo pants, and tugged at the part that slightly overlapped, uncertain how it opened. As she pulled, the ripping sound told her it was a hook and loop closure, so she yanked the two sides apart, freeing his impressive, engorged cock.

Phoebe admired it for a moment before she squatted, taking his pants down to the floor. She pushed them aside as he obliged her by stepping out of them and his unusual boots. With his long thick cock at eye level, she went on her knees and stroked its silky length with her hands. Gripping it just behind the tip, she licked off a drop of precum and drew her cheek from root to end on one side and then the other.

Blaze growled when she was about to take the head into her mouth. He gripped her upper arms and pulled her up to stand in front of him. "I want to cum in your cunt the first time," he said huskily.

He scooped her up and laid her on the bed without turning it down. Gently pushing her legs apart, he crawled onto the bed, knelt between them, and lowered himself over her.

As he held most of his weight on his arms and legs, Phoebe caressed his cheeks and ran her hands down over his neck, shoulders, and back. A wave of affection and gratitude made her want to give him whatever he wanted.

She was wet and ready to take him if that's what he wanted. It wasn't.

He started at her mouth with a deep sensual

kiss that sent waves of sweet desire to her breasts and her clit. Their tongues dueled in an erotic dance as she arched her back to rub her tender nipples against his chest.

Her clit throbbed for attention making her squirm beneath him. Hugging him and caressing his back, Phoebe made kitten sounds in her throat while Blaze plundered her mouth. The unseen nanites were like tiny bubbles bursting over and around her lips and tongue.

By the time he ended the kiss, her whole body clamored for him to fill her with his impressive cock.

That wasn't his plan.

He dragged his mouth down her jawline to her neck pressing little kisses to her skin, tasting and nibbling. He teased his way around her breast, driving her mad with need. She groaned with relief when his mouth closed over her nipple, and he sucked on it. She held his head there and crooned softly as the bolts of desire shot straight to her clit.

She breathed out soft little sighs and alternately panted. Tremors of need for release washed through her body in waves, and Blaze continued his sweet torment. From her breasts, he continued down her body, kissing and nibbling her smooth skin.

As he went lower on her belly and she guessed his intent, she gasped intermittently, anticipating the excruciating pleasure. She cried out and tried to buck her hips when his mouth covered her most sensitive bud. He flicked his tongue over and around it, then back and forth.

Before she could come, he backed off and drew his tongue up through her slit, feasting on her juices. Wrapping his hands around her thighs, he drew them wider apart, licking and sucking.

Phoebe crooned ohs and ahs, unable to string a coherent thought into words. She fisted the bed cover with each hand as her muscles tensed, coiled in anticipation of the stroke that would send her sailing over the summit of ecstasy.

With the first contraction of her climax, she screamed Blaze's name and a series of ahs. She gave him complete discretion until she became too sensitive. Then, she pushed his head back.

"I'm good."

Blaze turned his head and laid his cheek against her belly above her mons while aftershocks of her orgasm shook them both.

When she quieted, he raised up on his hands and knees, wiped his mouth on his forearm, and lowered himself over her body.

"Are you ready for me, my female?"

"I am," she smiled and caressed his face, spreading her legs wider with her knees drawn up to cradle his hips between her thighs.

He dragged the head of his cock up through her slick channel and pressed it against her sensitized clit. A new shudder of pleasure racked her body.

As he slid his cock into the hilt, he lowered himself onto her body with a sigh. He finally understood the concept of home, something he never had. Home was the female he'd waited for all his life. It was Phoebe.

He kissed her long and slow, then started pumping in and out of her body. Each time he drove into her, she raised her hips to welcome him, running her hands up and down his back. She looked up at him, watching his face as he accelerated his thrusts until he was pounding into her.

Blaze was giving himself, hard and deep,

hitting her sweet spot almost every time. It seemed like so much more than just a joining of their bodies. As they stared into each other's eyes, it felt like a joining of souls.

How could anyone treat this man like a machine? A commodity to be used and discarded. His enhancements didn't make him less of a man.

She could hardly fathom what it must have been like for him to spend nearly a century at war, going on the most dangerous missions. To be tortured for months...

Her own torment had only lasted days. All just fleeting thoughts quickly vanquished by the pleasure of Blaze's body, slamming his hips against hers and driving his cock deep into her.

Soon, she felt the familiar tightening, coiling low in her belly. Every thrust took her closer and closer. "Oh... Ah... You feel... So good." Then, she drawled several ah's as he took her over the top.

She knew he couldn't stop yet. She just closed her eyes and let herself feel everything about the man in her arms, writhing beneath him. Almost as soon as one climax ended, a second racked her body. She slid her hands low on his back, huffing as he drilled her.

Just as the third orgasm racked her body, Blaze roared as she took him over the summit with her. The power of their mutual climax was like nothing she had experienced before as his thrusts slowed and his cock throbbed inside her, shooting hot semen against her womb.

His lips found hers in a sweet, tender kiss.

"Now, you are mine, and I am yours...as long as we both live."

Phoebe was in awe as he said the words, hyper-aware of his big body on her and in her. She didn't yet comprehend that this was the cyborg way. But she could see that he meant it. From the moment she met him, he didn't seem like a man who said anything he didn't mean. She could see in his eyes that he was waiting for her to repeat it back. He needed to hear those words from her.

"Now, you are mine, and I am yours as long as we both live." Phoebe knew she meant the words as she said them, but to herself, she said: *If you don't turn into the monster, Martin Stone did.*

"I am not like him!" Blaze asserted in a soft, deadly tone.

He must have seen the hint of doubt flicker

in her eyes. She could see that hurt him.

Phoebe brought one hand up and caressed his cheek. "I'm making progress. After him, I swore I'd never let another man touch me again. And I made an exception for *you*."

That made him smile and drop a swift kiss on her lips.

NINE

"Oh!" Phoebe exclaimed as Blaze pulled out of her. "That tickly feeling in my mouth is down there, too."

"Yes, that's how it works." He got up from the bed she assumed to use the bathroom, but he scooped her up in his arms and carried her in with him. "How do you feel about breeding in the shower?" He looked at her, hopefully.

She was contemplating sleep but having him again put that thought right out of her mind. And she really did need to bathe.

Despite the diminutive size of the cabin, the shower easily fit them both inside. The walls and the floor were made from stone tile with a central AI that Blaze could ping from his onboard computer. Otherwise, it responded to voice commands.

Warm water trickled down on them when he stepped inside, and he set her down. He reached for a cloth and a bar of lavender soap. Wetting the washcloth, he rubbed it with the soap until it was laden with the scented suds.

He offered Phoebe the bar. "Would you

like to wash your hair while I wash the rest of you?"

"Sure." She gave him a demure smile; confident he knew she could wash her own body. He just wanted to explore her some more, but she didn't mind. She already knew he was damn good at foreplay. As she started rubbing the soap on her wet hair, he went down on one knee, putting her breasts at mouth level.

Before he did any washing, he suckled each nipple at length, making it hard for her to concentrate on what she was doing. When she finally got her hair thoroughly sudsy, he started washing her all over, lingering at her pussy and her breasts longer than necessary. She chuckled as he did, enjoying his attention. It was nice to be pampered.

Once he had finished soaping her body, he apparently commanded the water to flow faster to rinse her. When it went back to the slight drizzle, Phoebe held out her hand to him. "My turn to wash you."

He handed her the cloth, and she rubbed the soap on it for more suds, then gave it to him to wash his hair. Before she started washing him, she stepped forward and kissed him in the middle of his chest. His blatantly engorged cock poking against her belly made her core clench and her breasts ache for more attention.

Blaze's physique was mouthwatering; she wanted to kiss him all over. Her irresistible attraction to him gave credence to his claim that she was his genetic mate. Phoebe never felt desire this intense in her limited experience with men.

She kissed her way across to his male nipples in turn, licking and sucking them. He gave a sexy growl as she did. Moving behind him, she soaped his back with the coarse cloth, lingering over his tight ass. She finished his legs and moved to the front, starting at his shoulders and down.

Phoebe held out her hand to Blaze for the soap when she was ready to wash his male parts. She went down on one knee, used her hands to soap his cock and scrotum. That elicited more sexy growls. The water flow increased again and washed the suds away.

She took his cock between her hands and stroked it fondly. Kissing the head and lapping at it with her tongue, she took it into her mouth and sucked on it.

Blaze took that for about a minute before he lifted her up and pressed her against the tile wall. Leaning into her, he crushed her luscious breasts against his chest and claimed her mouth in a deep, passionate kiss. She lifted her legs to wrap them around his hips and put her arms around his shoulders. He slid his cock into her, and she moaned into his mouth.

He was all alpha male, holding her captive to his desires. It was incredibly arousing, knowing he only wanted her and no one else. He'd explained that his conditioning made him unable to lie, and certainly not about what she meant to him. He could only withhold the information.

The pleasure was so exquisite when he filled her with his cock, it left her breathless for a few seconds. He pulled away from the wall, cupping her buttocks when he started pumping in and out of her.

He started with slow, hard, deep thrusts, rubbing the flesh above his cock against her clit. Holding her mouth captive to his kiss, she could only hum her enjoyment.

"Blaze..." she murmured his name when she could talk. "You feel... So... Good."

By then, he was ravishing her hard and fast. Phoebe gave all that he asked with his body; her gratification was so great. This time they reached climax together, and they both exclaimed, "mine!"

Blaze held her kissing, nuzzling, and caressing, in no hurry to separate from her. "I'm so glad I found you," he whispered close to her ear."

"Me, too." She whispered back and thought to herself, this cyborg was a man she could love.

TEN

Pain. Phoebe's shoulders ached as though her arms had been pulled from the sockets. Her throat was raw and her mouth so dry she couldn't swallow.

When she opened her eyes, the room was dimly lit with a sliver of fading sunlight let in by a glass block in the wall. A bitter sob broke through as she realized she was still in the dungeon. It was a secret room in Martin Stone's basement.

She discovered it by accident. She had never seen anything like it, so she asked Martin what it was for. He said it was an adult playroom, told her not to worry. If she behaved, she would never see the inside of it.

According to Martin, she hadn't. Talking and smiling at one of his men just a little too long set him off in a rage. He didn't care when she insisted that it was completely innocent. Martin asserted that the man wanted her. Then he accused her of sleeping with the man when she asked about her horse because he oversaw the stable.

That's how she came to be hanging from the ceiling by her wrists naked in this horrible room. Her whole body was on fire from dozens of narrow welts. Martin had beat her with the thick switch for what seemed hours. It went on for days. Phoebe couldn't remember whether it was three or four.

She had screamed until she had no voice left, and she'd passed out before the last beating was finished. Instead of putting her back in the cage as he had before, Martin left her hanging there. Was that because he was going to kill her this time?

How could she ever think this man loved her? Or that she loved him? He was a monster. He hadn't just beat her; he raped her. But forcing sex was less traumatic than the torture. She had been a willing partner before he turned evil on her. Trying to talk him down got her a hard slap in the face.

How am I ever going to get out of this? She wondered miserably.

A sound from the door made her gasp, worried that he'd come back to kill her.

"Oh, dearie. What has he done to you?"

Martin's housekeeper had come carrying an oil lamp.

"Sara, he's crazy!" she rasped hoarsely. "Said I dishonored him by flirting with the stableman. Please help me."

"Oh, my! I'm not even supposed to be in here, but I heard crying."

"Please, Sara. I swear, I will never tell him. I'm going home and never coming back."

The housekeeper took her down, and Phoebe crumpled to the floor in a sobbing heap.

Sara brought her a cup of water, and she took it gratefully. "Where are your clothes?"

"Ruined. He tore them and cut them off. My shoes are all that's left."

"Drink your water, and I will see what I can find, hanging in the laundry room."

"Be careful; I don't want you to get in trouble," Phoebe said hoarsely. "I know how badly you need this job."

"Don't worry, he is playing poker with his cronies. He will be busy until the wee hours," Sara told her as she hurried from the room."

Phoebe was so weak, she crawled across the cement floor to where Martin had tossed her worn sneakers the first day. A couple of minutes later, Sara came back with a pair of pants and shirt that Phoebe recognized as her own.

"I'm sorry they are still damp, but with the rain yesterday, I hung them inside."

"It's okay; better than naked," Phoebe rasped. She got up slowly from the floor by a supreme effort of will.

"Oh, my God!" Sara muttered. "He did that, to you?" Even the weak light from the setting sun and the oil lamp couldn't hide the welts that covered her body from her neck and arms to the tops of her feet. Her face was the only place he hadn't hit her, except with his hand.

"Uh-huh," was all she could manage as she leaned against the wall and held out her hand for one of the garments.

Sara offered the worn cotton tunic, waited for her to don it, and then handed her the drawstring cotton pants. The cool dampness felt good on the burn of all the welts. Pushing her sore feet into the slip-on sneakers, she stood leaning against the wall.

Phoebe felt a little better since drinking the water. But she was having a hard time staying on her feet. She wasn't even sure she could ride, let alone saddle her horse.

"I need to get my horse… Need to get away."

"Oh, sweetheart, you're in no condition to go anywhere. When it's completely dark, I will take you to my house. You can stay there for a few days until you're strong enough. He would never come there looking for you."

Sara had been a good friend for the months that she had been there. She had come to hate Martin Stone as much as Phoebe had. But Sara was widowed and had two children to support. She bartered her housekeeping duties for food and credits for clothing.

She'd warned Phoebe to stay on Martin's good side. Now, she realized that Martin had done this before.

"He killed the others, didn't he?"

Sara pressed her lips into a thin line, closing her eyes, and nodded. "I hoped it would be different for you. He seemed to dote on you so much more than the others. But, when I hadn't seen you in two days, I got worried."

"And no one ever heard me screaming?" Phoebe rasped.

"I think this room must keep the sound in."

A short while later, they left through the

83

exterior basement door with only the moonlight to guide their way. Sara put her arm around Phoebe's waist, and Phoebe put her arm around Sara's shoulders. They walked that way for the two blocks to Sara's house.

Sara's eldest daughter was horrified when she saw her mother helping Phoebe into their house. Her younger daughter was already in bed.

"We're going to put her on the daybed in the old nursery," said Sara. "You will tell no one she is here, Joanie. Her life depends on it."

Joanie knew the stories of the things Martin Stone did. It was all Sara could do sometimes to hide her hatred for him and speak to him in a subservient civil tone.

"I wish you could quit that job," Joanie grumbled.

"He would make sure no one else hired you or me. Someday, he'll cross the wrong person, and he will be gone. I just hope the next guy who takes his place isn't worse."

Sara and Joanie helped Phoebe walk into the nursery and onto the narrow bed. "You rest, and I will bring you some soup."

Finally, when she was alone, she buried her face in the pillow and sobbed her heart out until she fell into a restless sleep only to wake up screaming because she dreamed Martin had found her.

Blaze woke the second that Phoebe started to stir restlessly in his arms. Although he didn't need to sleep for days, he was happy to hold his female and doze. The pheromones caused her to breed with him even though she was nearly exhausted.

Those pheromones were too powerful to let her sleep without consummating their mating. Blaze sighed as he looped the memory of every detail. Breeding with her was every bit as glorious as he could ever have dreamt. He would cherish the memory for the rest of his life.

Phoebe stirred just a little at first, then she started to whimper. Then she began to struggle, letting out a scream that ended in a series of sobs.

"Phoebe, Phoebe, wake up," Blaze rumbled. "It's a dream. You're safe. You're safe!" He gave her a gentle shake and patted her cheek.

Her eyes flew open, and she tried to push

him away. "Let me go! I hate you! Let me go."

He crooned her name a few times and said, "It's me, Blaze, you're safe."

Right after that, her fist smashed into the side of his face. It smarted a little, but it was no worse than a slap.

"Ow," she cried, opening her eyes wide. "Omigod, omigod, Blaze..."

With his metal-infused skeleton, he knew it hurt her way more than him. "It's okay, sweet mate. You could not hurt me with that little punch." His eyes darkened as he frowned. "You were dreaming about him, weren't you?"

"Yes," and she wept softly, choking back sobs. "He's a fucking sadist, and he has this dungeon. He made it like a game at first, then I made him mad. When I said the safe word, he ignored it. He... he hit me..." Phoebe broke into sobs as he held her and rocked her in his arms.

It hurt his heart to hear her broken sobs between her words as she told him about the beatings and escape. The horror of it enraged him.

Blaze would take great pleasure in killing him, slowly inflicting as much agony as possible. The Mesaarkans had educated him on all the ways to inflict pain on a human without killing him.

That's how Martin Stone was going to die.

ELEVEN

"I'm sorry; I didn't intend to dump all that on you. I thought I was okay… I *was* all right until Martin had them burn my house and kill my animals," she mused as Blaze held her on his lap, stroking her hair.

"It's healthier that you let it out because keeping the pain inside only works for a while… Until something happens that starts a chain reaction that paralyzes you with hurt and anger." He caressed her cheek and tucked her hair behind her ear. "The nanites I shared with you will help level out your brain chemistry. If that's not enough, I'll contact the Medical Center in New Chicago for a more precise diagnosis and treatment."

"If it weren't for Sara, I probably would have died there. I hope he never found out… And she is all right."

"I'll check on her when I go to Grafton for recon. Martin Stone's reign over the town will soon be coming to an end," Blaze assured her, putting his arms around her and planting a light kiss on her forehead.

"They will try to kill you."

"Better humanoids than Stone have tried. He will learn that I don't kill that easy. What kind of weapons do they have?"

"Guns with bullets."

"They won't pierce my armor."

"When will you go?" she asked uneasily.

"It can wait a week or two until you are feeling better."

Phoebe sighed contentedly. "You made me feel better, a lot better last night."

"You made me feel joy for the first time in my life. More happiness than I ever felt killing the Mesaarkans in the war." His tone bordered on reverence.

Phoebe pulled back from him and looked at him with a shocked expression. "You liked killing people?"

"They made us that way so that feel-good hormones pumped into our system when we killed the enemy."

"Who decides who is the enemy?"

"In the war, our commanders told us who to kill. I have since been re-educated for law enforcement. Now, I decide who I kill. Martin

Stone fits my criteria."

"You will get no argument from me," Phoebe asserted. "Sara told me he killed at least three women before I met him."

"After what he did to you and your property, he will die slowly," Blaze growled.

Phoebe shivered at the ferocity of his tone, realizing she liked Blaze's plan a little too much.

"Don't let it bother you. Who could blame you for liking the idea?" Blaze said as though he had read her mind.

Then she smiled at him for the first time since she woke from the nightmare. As she looked into his midnight blue eyes, his admiring gaze was impossible to ignore. Their pheromones made the attraction too potent to resist.

But there was tenderness within his passion for her. She couldn't forget how he helped her get the animals she had left and get them settled. He understood that it was crucial to her, so it became necessary for him.

They were both still naked from the night before. The way he looked at her made her nipples tightened into stiff peaks, prickling for attention while her core clenched as wet heat gathered between her thighs. Adding to the fire, his cock was hard against her bottom.

As he breathed in, he smiled, and she knew he had scented her desire. "You wish to breed." It was a statement, not a question.

"Do you wish to breed?" she asked sassily as though his blatant erection hadn't already answered the question.

She didn't wait for him to answer, rolling off his lap and the bed and climbing back on, facing him.

"I wish it very much," he said, the head of his cock at already found its way into her wet entrance. "All I need to want you is to think about you like this, and my cock is ready."

"Me too. I never wanted a man like I want you."

Blaze gripped her waist and drew her to him until his cock was fully seated inside her. Phoebe was straddling him with her legs folded under her. She wound her arms around his neck as he hugged her against him and pressed his mouth to hers.

He was an artist when it came to kissing. His full lips were surprisingly soft, and he knew just how to tease her tongue so that exquisite sensations of carnal delight surged to her core. As he kissed her long and slow and deep, he pressed her tightly to him, her breasts squeezed against his hard chest. Altogether, it made her core clench and unclench around his hard cock inside her.

When Blaze ended the kiss, he tipped her back to give special attention to her luscious breasts. She rested her hands on his muscular upper arms while he took one nipple into his mouth and suckled it thoroughly. He gave the other the same treatment while she crooned her pleasure and squirmed, rubbing her clit against his pubis.

His attentions made her come spontaneously in a release so intense that she threw her head back and wailed ecstatically. Blaze smiled indulgently at her pleasure as he pulled her back against him, kissing her lips deeply.

Phoebe put her arms around his neck and shoulders, kissing him back with abandon, still shuddering with orgasm. While kissing her, he rolled her over on her back, so he was cradled against her pelvis.

"How would you like it, my female? Slow and easy or hard and fast?"

"Take me how you need me," she said

happily. "I want you to feel as good as you make me feel. I just know I want you more."

"Slow and easy to start, then hard and fast to the end."

Phoebe laughed and kissed him. Things were happening so fast between them, but she found him utterly irresistible. It was easy to put the bad things that had happened to her in the background when she was in his arms having mind-blowing sex.

True to his word, Blaze started slow and easy and steadily increase the power and speed of his thrusts until he was pounding into her, taking her to a level of exhilarating pleasure she had never known before. Part of the time, she closed her eyes and simply felt him moving on top of her, driving his hard cock deep into her core, caressing that sweet spot with nearly every thrust. Then she would open her eyes, and she saw him watching her face as he slammed his pelvis into hers again and again.

Nothing else seemed to exist except the two of them joined in pursuit of sexual bliss. It made Phoebe believe his assertion that she was his genetic mate. She was certain no one else could ever fuck her the way Blaze did.

She didn't know how many times she came

or if it was one long orgasm until he found his release. As he pulsed inside her, shooting his hot semen into her, she had another powerful orgasm, keening loudly as Blaze roared.

Then he collapsed on top of her, careful to keep his superior weight from crushing her while pressing tightly against her. Phoebe hugged him with her arms and legs, wanting to keep him inside her as long as possible. A rush of emotion filled her with tenderness for the big cyborg.

No other man had been so cognizant of her needs nor made such efforts to satisfy them.

Phoebe could hardly fathom how he had dropped into her life just when she needed him. And she liked him, and the way that he treated her like she was precious to him. This time she didn't feel like it was too good to last.

There had been signs with Martin, but he had played it so smooth in the beginning that she let them slide. She thought she needed him so she didn't see the cracks in the facade he put on for her.

Phoebe mentally shook herself. She surely didn't want to think about that cruel bastard with her body wrapped around Blaze. Still, she couldn't quite shake the hint of doubt reminding her that she had been wrong about men before. She shoved it back to where it came from.

None of them were cyborgs claiming to be her genetic match. She wanted what was happening between them to be as real as it seemed more than anything.

TWELVE

"Commander Dark? Captain Blaze Savage reporting, sir."

"Go ahead, Savage."

"I've found my female. She is Phoebe Brooks of Texas, and I have claimed her."

"Of course, you would like some more time to get acquainted with her. Blaze, no one deserves time with their female more than you."

"Say two weeks?"

"More if you wish."

"Considering what Phoebe endured at the hands of a so-called mayor, I shouldn't delay more than that."

"And you're going to remove him?"

"Permanently. Martin Stone tortured her… and he has killed other females. That is my first mission. But I can't take my female, and I don't want to leave her unprotected."

"I can send the newbie Javen Black. He is a trained protector, and he has asked to be assigned to your service."

"Do you think he will be happy with just protecting my female?"

"He will do whatever you need him to do until you are ready to assign him a protector position. He was doing agricultural support while waiting for a protector position."

"I will contact him when I am ready to take Martin Stone."

"His duties here are flexible, so you can have him when you need him."

"Thank you, sir."

"You're welcome. Congratulations, Savage. Out."

Savage out."

Blaze's attention snapped back to the scene in front of him. Most of the land surrounding his cabin had been reclaimed by the wild. The grass among the clumps of trees was tall, with saplings and bushes interspersed.

When he was awarded the property, he hadn't thought what he would do with it. He was mainly concerned with the cabin and the yard that had been carved out of the wilderness. Perhaps his female would have some ideas. Her homestead had been well established, but Stone had ruined it for her. It made him angry after learning what else he had done to her.

He'd awakened before dawn and spend a long time just watching Phoebe sleep. She was so beautiful, and she was his. He would destroy anyone who tried to take her from him, and he would kill the man who hurt her.

When she woke, he would bring her nourishment and help her care for her animals. She clearly cherished them, so he would value them too.

"Blaze?"

Her voice pulled him from his thoughts instantly and set him in motion almost as quickly.

"I'm here, Phee." He sat down on the bed beside her.

She sat up, forgetting she was naked. She started to cover her breasts, then stopped. "You went outside naked?"

He shrugged. "No one is out there to see me, and you have already seen it all."

Phoebe giggled and blushed.

Blaze leaned over and kissed her cheek. "Are you ready for breakfast, my mate?"

"I would love some after I hit the lav." She slid over to the other side of the bed and got up. "I will meet you at the table."

Blaze couldn't help smiling as Phoebe padded toward the dining table naked a few minutes later. He immediately went hard at the delicious sight. She was deliberately not looking there.

Breakfast was fruit juice and meal bars, the same as supper the previous evening. Blaze had opened both meal bars by the time Phoebe joined him at the table. She picked hers up and started eating it without comment.

"After we finish eating, I need to feed the animals and let Sherry out to pasture."

"As I expected. Then we can decide how to improve their quarters."

"Too bad we couldn't move my barn here."

"We can have one delivered and have it assembled here," Blaze told her.

"Are you sure about this? Are you that sure about *us*, that you won't regret changing things around...? If... Things don't work out for us?"

"Yes, I am sure. I am your male, and I will always be. What things do you think won't work out?" Blaze frowned.

"You say that now, but you could change someday."

"That's not the cyborg way. There is almost *nothing* I wouldn't do for you. All you have to do is ask."

As she looked into his eyes, she believed him. "And if I want to leave you?"

"Do you want to?"

"No. I'm just saying '*If.*'"

"I don't plan to make you want that." He reached across the table, caressing her cheek with his fingers. "We have said the mating vows. They don't end if we disagree. We will work it out. I am genetically programmed only for you."

"So, you are my *husband*? Just like that?"

"Yes, for as long as I live."

"And that will be a long time."

"With the nanites I give you, it will be."

"How do you know *I* will make *you* happy?"

"You already do." Blaze smiled at her.

Phoebe caught her breath as a shock of want rippled through her and fluttered between her thighs. Her nipples tightened, and Blaze's smile brightened. Her cheeks heated.

"You are even more desirable when your face gets pink." He leaned across the table and gave her a light kiss on her lips. "I want to breed with you again, too."

"After the animals are fed and watered," she insisted.

"I can wait. I will help you."

"Just like that. What do you know about caring for animals?" She took another bite of her meal bar. It tasted vaguely like meat, mildly sweet and salty at the same time.

Blaze recited the care and feeding requirements for horses, goats, dogs, and chickens while Phoebe finished eating. He even mentioned a few things she didn't know.

"How do you know all that?"

"I downloaded it from the Enclave's AI archives. That's how I knew to get fencing and feed for them."

"Thank you for doing this."

"Cyborgs all know that our lives will change when we find our genetic mates. Then, we have to work out how our lives can fit together."

"All I know is homesteading. My family

101

has done it for generations."

"Do you want to continue homesteading? We can do that here." Blaze said. "I want you to do the work that you enjoy."

"Yes, I never thought of doing anything else." She got up from the table. "I'm going to get dressed."

Blaze sighed and closed his eyes for a moment, thinking about weapons maintenance to take his mind off breeding his female. He knew watching her walk away would only make his need worse. But waiting could also enhance their pleasure when they did finally come together.

There were no feed boxes for the horse and the goats and only one bucket in the shed. Phoebe gave the bucket to the horse with an estimated amount of grain, and Blaze found a plastic panel for the goats' feed and one for the chickens. They used a folded tarp for the dog's food.

"They all came to you when they saw you. The animals seem to like you." Blaze said as he watched her greet them.

"Partly, they like that I bring them food. But Brandy is a companion as well as a working dog."

"When we go inside, we can order the food receptacles for your animals. I didn't think of that when I ordered the rest of the things."

Phoebe smiled and nodded.

By the time the other animals were fed, Sherry had finished her morning ration and was ready to go out to pasture. The mother and baby goats went as well.

Since they were outside, Blaze decided to take the time to look at his property and show Phoebe around. As they walked, they talked and got to know each other a little better.

Although she never had formal schooling, Phoebe's family had books in their home handed down from generation to generation. Some were old school books, and others were about survival without the infrastructure that the Mesaarkans destroyed in their initial bombing throughout the entire world.

Even before the Mesaarkans, there were worries that public utilities would fail and people would be left to fend for themselves. Growing numbers of people chose to live off the grid and become self-sufficient, growing their own food, and using renewable energy. That was the legacy of Phoebe's family line. Her education came from the accumulation of paper books. She could read and write, do math, and understood much science.

"Losing all my family's books was almost worse than losing the house," Phoebe told him.

"I can't get those back for you, but I can get you a tablet so that you can access millions of books archived by the Enclave."

"A tablet? Like paper?" Phoebe frowned.

"It's personal tech for people who don't have onboard tech like cyborgs do."

"What exactly is this Enclave?"

"They are part of an international group of world survival preppers. They started almost two centuries ago after Earth developed interstellar capability. Speculating on the possibility of an interstellar attack, they developed cyborgs to defend Earth and the Federation and explore space for worlds to develop and colonize. But not every corporation wanted cyborgs in their crews; we would have known better than to murder alien civilians with a prior claim to a valuable planet. Once the war started, they couldn't make us fast enough."

THIRTEEN

"What do you mean?" They had stopped walking for a moment, and she turned to face him.

"We were not invincible even though we are hard to kill... And we were expendable. A half million or more of us died because they could always make more. The promise of finding their one genetic mate never came to fruition for those soldiers. That was the cause they died for."

Phoebe looked at him with tears in her eyes, aching for the cyborgs who lost their lives without ever knowing love.

"The Mesaarkans had made me wish for death many times, but I found the strength to stay alive with the promise of finding you." Blaze cupped her cheek with his hand and wiped away the single tear with his thumb. "Now, I am so glad I did."

Phoebe grasped his hand and turned her face to kiss his palm. "I am, too."

Then they were kissing passionately, their hands running all over each other. Phoebe found herself holding on to a tree trunk with her only pair of pants pooled by her left foot and Blaze taking her from behind.

As she keened at his hard, fast pounding, he worried that he was too rough with her. Three times he asked if she were okay.

"Don't stop!" she cried. "Don't stop! I need you... need this."

As he was getting close, he merely rubbed her clit a few strokes, and she came hard screaming, "Yes, ah yes Blaze!"

And he came, too. As the orgasm played out, he reached under her shirt and pinched her nipples, making her shudder with a new series of contractions around his pulsing cock. Being inside her like that was utter bliss.

Bad as the Mesaarkans tortured him, breeding with Phoebe was at the opposite of the spectrum in pleasure. Blaze enjoyed their connection at length before he finally withdrew from her.

As he straightened, she stayed bent against the tree while his excess semen dripped out onto the ground. Blaze hadn't thought to bring a cloth to clean her; he hadn't been thinking about breeding when they started their walk. But he quickly realized that was the case with spontaneous breeding.

"I'm sorry, sweet mate, I didn't think about afterward," he said.

She giggled and said, "I didn't either, but it was so… Good." She balanced against the tree, picked up the waist of her pants, slipped her foot into the left pant leg and pulled them up. "I guess I will have to wash them out and be naked until they dry."

Blaze couldn't resist framing her face in his hands to steal a slow, tender kiss from her lips. "I don't see that as a hardship," he deadpanned when he lifted his mouth from hers.

"Of course, you wouldn't," she gave him a cheeky grin.

A subtle whine overhead drew their attention.

"The things I ordered should be on that drone tram. We should get back to the cabin."

"What did you order?" she asked.

"You will see." He took her hand and led her to the path back to the cabin.

When they got to the cabin, a medium-size shipping container was sitting at the front door. Blaze picked it up and carried it to the door, and Phoebe jogged ahead and opened the conventional door for him. Inside he set it on the floor in front of the living room sofa and pressed his thumb to the ID plate on top, and the split top opened.

He took out a small thin, rectangular item. "This is your personal communication device as well as a holographic computer." He unfolded four sections that melded into a seamless flat screen. "I'll show you how to use it after you see what else I have for you."

He pulled out a bundle of folded khaki green t-shirts like the ones he wore, handing them to her. "Since you literally lost everything but the clothes you were wearing, I put in a request for clothing. These are standard issue, and we have some black cargo pants and boots like mine in your size. They come from the automated factory that makes clothing for the cyborgs.

"Thank you, Blaze. It's so sweet of you to think of it," she said sincerely. "I didn't know how I could replace the clothing I lost in the fire. There were a couple of shops in Grafton that make cloth from cotton and made clothes…"

"But you can't go there for obvious reasons," he said.

"No. It doesn't matter. These will suit me just fine." She smiled at him, then frowned at his serious expression. "What is it?"

"In a few more days, I have to go to Grafton and start the work I came here to do."

"When?"

"Next week, Monday."

Phoebe gave him a distressed look, and he sat down beside her and put his arm around her. "You will be safe here. Commander Dark is sending me the newbie Javen Black to keep watch here."

"A newbie?"

"It's what we call the cyborgs who were never awakened for the war. There were about 12,000 of them when the commander came back to Earth."

"I don't need a bodyguard. I can take care of myself," she said indignantly. "And I have Brandy. She will let me know if anyone comes."

"Phoebe, don't fight me on this. I won't be able to do my job if I am looping worry for your safety," he said. "These last two weeks have been the best in my life. I would love to just stay here and help turn this place into a homestead. There will be times I can but I can't be with you all the time."

"Who's going to protect you? Stone has thirty or forty men in his gang. You are only one cyborg. How can you fight all of them?"

Blaze leaned over to pull one more item from the shipping container. "With this."

He held up a belt with a small rectangular panel attached to it. At her puzzled expression, he stood and stepped back, hooking the belt around him just above his hipbones. He pinged the device at the small of his back. Almost instantly, it covered his body with silvery black armor that made him look like a robot to Phoebe.

Her mouth dropped open. "How?"

"Nanites and a metallic polymer assemble my nearly invincible new armor on demand." As quickly as it had compiled on his body, it receded. "This new intelligent armor is far superior to anything we had in the war."

Blaze took off the belt, hung it in his arms locker, and then came back and pulled out one more thing from the crate. "You said you wanted to start a new garden." He handed her a thick packet with pictures of vegetables and herbs on it. It's the same seed packet the enclave gives out to people who reclaim abandoned properties, so they can grow their own food."

"Thank you, Blaze. This is great. The only thing is; I need tools to get the soil ready. My old ones probably burned with the house---at least the handles. I kept them leaning against the house by the back porch."

"The newbie Javen Black is bringing a bot-tiller on loan along with a rake, hoe, pick, and shovel. Did I leave anything out?"

"I don't think so." Phoebe jumped up from the couch and threw her arms around his neck, planting a swift kiss on his lips.

The feel of her lush curves plastered against him was all it took to make him hard, and he growled low and sexy. Pressing his mouth to hers, he initiated a deeper, more arousing kiss, eliciting kitten sounds from her as she kissed him back.

"I think I need to take you in the shower, so you can put your new clothes on," he said with a lascivious smirk.

"Mm," she smiled up at him.

He scooped her up into his arms and carried her there.

FOURTEEN

The next week and a half passed all too quickly. One day blended into the next as they began falling in love while learning to live together. Blaze didn't want to leave Phoebe any more than she wanted him to go.

He waited to leave that day until Javen arrived. Although it was doubtful that anyone associated with Martin Stone would find his remote cabin, someone else might. He had heard the horror stories about gangers coming from the ruined cities, looking for females to abduct. He wasn't taking any chances with Phoebe.

Lastly, before he left, he said, "It might be a couple of days or more before I get back."

"Okay," Phoebe said. "Just be careful and come back to me in one piece."

"I intend to." Blaze stroked her cheek with his fingertips. Leaving her was harder than he expected, then he reminded himself what he was going to do. It had been years since he had killed any beings. He was still a product of his conditioning. Killing released endorphins into his system, not unlike those released during sex though not quite as potent.

"I'll be back as soon as I can." He turned and stalked to his sky cycle, climbed on, and set off skyward without looking back. His next stop was Martin Stone's residence.

#

Before he left for duty, Blaze and Phoebe chose the food garden spot and staked out the plot. Blaze greeted Javen on his way to mount his sky cycle. They had already gone over the instructions through the cyborg network.

Phoebe watched him climb on the cycle and take off before she greeted Javen. She gave Javen a friendly smile and said, "Hello."

Javen dipped his head respectfully and said hello, and met her glance briefly. He seemed a little uncomfortable in her presence.

"As promised, I have brought a sod breaker and bot tiller to clear and till the ground within the specified coordinates," he recited. "When these machines finish, you will only have to plant."

"Are there no bots for planting?"

"Only for large scale planting. The planters are attachments to the droid tractors. They are suited only to planting whole fields in a single crop."

"We would only need something like that to plant more pasture if the grass growing there isn't good enough."

"I will examine the grasses in the area Captain Savage specified to extend the pasture. I will also check for poisonous flora."

"The land has been unattended for decades before Blaze got here. That's probably a good idea."

Javen went silent and fixed his attention on the sod breaker as it peeled and rolled the grass from the garden plot. Every few minutes, he scanned the sky and the surrounding land for intruders. Hardly anything around was moving except a few birds and rabbits and Phoebe's own animals.

It quickly became apparent that Javen was there to do a job and was not comfortable making friendly conversation. Maybe it was protocol not to be too familiar to his superior's female. It was also not in a cyborg's makeup to be attracted to any female but his genetic mate.

Phoebe watched the sod breaker for a few minutes, then went to feed the animals and let them out into the pasture. When she finished, she drifted back to watch the progress on the garden plot. The sod breaker had cleared a quarter of the ground, and the bot tiller started turning over and loosening the soil.

She was impressed by the way the two bots were timed to follow each other. That job would have taken weeks with a pick and shovel. The bots would finish by the end of the day. The bot tiller also fed the soil as it tilled so she would be able to start planting in a day or two.

#

About an hour later, Blaze set his sky craft down in a wooded area just outside town behind some brush to camouflage it. With the cockpit closed, only he could open it with his biosignature.

Phoebe had told him how to find Stone's house which was where he conducted all his business. Stone usually had four or five of his lackeys for security, all armed with guns and knives. Blaze would not be intimidated by thugs with only those weapons.

Blaze decided just to take his knives in his

vest and sidearm and leave his ion rifle. It was unwieldy in small spaces such as inside a house.

As he walked the residential street toward Stone's place, he noted that every two or three houses were abandoned. Before the war, Grafton was a busy town of twenty thousand or more. Now there were less than a third of that.

Even the houses that were occupied were in disrepair. Only a few looked unsalvageable. The neighborhood could be rehabilitated to provide housing to people from the ruins of bombed-out cities.

First, he would have to take back the town from Martin Stone and give it back to the people. Then the enclave could send in construction teams to renovate the houses and restore essential utilities.

One of those teams had done a beautiful job renovating the abandoned cabin appropriated for him. The Enclave team upgraded it with a home AI, more efficient solar panels, a windmill, and a security system.

Phoebe's directions were precise, and he found Stone's house quickly. Just as she said, the big white house was in pristine condition outside, and soon he would see whether the inside matched.

Blaze stopped at the foot of the front steps and scanned the house for life forms. He noted five, marched up the stairs, and pounded on the door. As expected, one of Stone's underlings opened the door.

"Who are you, and what do you want?"

"Blaze Savage to see Martin Stone," he said evenly, ignoring his rude demeanor. He deliberately did not identify himself as an Enclave Ranger because what he planned would not be sanctioned by the council. Nor did he wear his badge on his vest either.

"He doesn't see anyone without an appointment," said the lackey, and he started to shut the door in his face.

Blaze stuck his foot in the doorway to stop it, pushed open the door, and grabbed the man by the throat, forcing him inside and lifting him, so his feet didn't touch the floor. He was nearly the same size as Blaze but was no match for him.

"He will see me," Blaze asserted as the man tried to pry his fingers from his throat. "Where is he?"

Blaze lowered him and eased the hold on his throat so he could speak. "Through the living room to the right, in his office."

"Mr. Stone is no longer in charge of this town. I am. If you leave now and pass the word to your cronies, I will let you live." Blaze gave his throat a slight squeeze to show the thug he could end him then and there. As soon as Blaze let go and stepped aside, the other man scurried out of the house, bounding down the steps, then running for his life.

Blaze then strolled through the lavishly furnished living room and into the opened office. Stone was absorbed in the ledger on his desk, so he didn't look up immediately when the cyborg came and stood in front of his polished wood desk.

Stone finally looked up a minute or two later. "Who let you in? What the fuck, do you want?" he grumbled in a snide tone. Then he bellowed, "Clade, Pete, Jesse, Tom, get in here now!"

Blaze stepped back beside the door at the faint sound of footsteps. Seconds later, the four men burst into the office, and the cyborg slammed the door closed behind them.

They turned around at the sound of the slamming door, facing Blaze. Seeing only a tall, brawny man without a weapon in hand, they didn't conceive any reason to fear him.

"Get rid of him," Stone commanded.

Blaze folded his arms across his chest and stared at them. "If you leave now, I will let you live."

"Yeah, what are you going to do all by yourself?"

Blaze moved so fast, he had one of them by the throat, raised up off the floor before they could react. "Who burned Phoebe's house and killed her livestock?"

Their friend's face was bright red, and he was struggling to breathe.

"Don't kill him! He's my brother. Mr. Stone ordered some of the men to do it to teach her a lesson."

Blaze released the man, who crumpled to the floor gasping and gagging. The one who called him brother, hurried to help him up to leave while another opened the wooden door and bolted. The brother half carried and half dragged his sibling from the room.

"You can leave, too," Blaze said to the man he recognized from the men chasing Phoebe, but they'd never been introduced. "Or I can end you right here."

That last man's hands fisted at his sides, and there was pure hatred in his eyes but he backed down. Backing out of the office, he ran from the house, slamming the front door behind him.

Meanwhile, Stone had pulled out a pistol and aimed it at the middle of Blaze's chest. The cyborg grabbed it just as Stone pulled the trigger, and the shot went wild. Stone's finger snapped as the gun was ripped from his grasp, and he screamed in pain.

Blaze gripped him by the front of his shirt with one hand and his throat with the other hand and pulled him up over the desk. Dragging him from his office, he looked for the door that Phoebe told him led to the basement and Martin Stone's sadistic 'playroom.' While he understood the practice of BDSM between consenting adults, what Stone had done to Phoebe was torture.

"W-what are you going to do?"

Blaze didn't answer. He gazed around the room and found the manacles hanging from the chains anchored to the ceiling. Dragging Stone across the concrete floor, he quickly fastened the other man's wrists in the manacles over his head.

He pulled a large military knife from one of the sheaths in his vest and showed it to Stone, then stroked his cheek with it without cutting him. He did the same thing over his throat. Stone shuddered.

"Phoebe told me what you did to her down here," Blaze told him in a deadly calm voice. "That's what I'm going to do to you."

"No, you can't. That was between her and me. She was into pain. She liked it."

Blaze went still, his razor-sharp knife inches from Stone's throat. He squeezed the handle so hard that it cracked. All it would take was a flick of his wrist to slice into the carotid artery, and Stone would bleed out in minutes.

"Liar!" Blaze backhanded him instead, careful not to knock him out. Otherwise, he wouldn't feel the pain, and Blaze wanted him to feel pain---for Phoebe and for the women he killed before her. He estimated the odds that Stone was planning to kill her at 97.089%. Failing that, he would be 99.99% likely to kill another female.

He wouldn't get the chance ever again.

Blaze took the knife and slit opened Stone's cotton tunic shirt down the front, nicking his chest with the point purposely. He went on cutting off the rest of Stone's hand-made clothing, nicking his flesh with nearly every cut. Stone whimpered and sniveled through most of it. Rivulets of blood ran down his body from all the shallow cuts.

When Stone hung naked from the chains where he'd hung Phoebe to torture her, Blaze browsed the room for the stick to whip him. There were a variety of different thicknesses of switches about four feet in length. Blaze chose one that was a half-inch in diameter and sturdy enough to complete the punishment

He landed the first blow on his back, and Stone screamed. He screamed with almost every blow after that. "Please, stop! Why are you doing this?"

"Did you stop when Phoebe begged? Did you stop when the other females begged?" Blaze hit him again. He systematically laid blows over his whole body, front, and back. Yet as he screamed through the pain, the sadistic bastard was aroused.

Blaze hit him there too. He finally stopped when Stone's whole body was covered with raised red welts with rivulets of blood running down his body. By then, the man was barely conscious and hung limply from the manacles on his wrists. Blaze returned the flogging stick to its place on the wall. He went back to Stone, grabbed him by the hair, tilted his head back, and stabbed him in the throat through his carotid artery.

As Stone bled out, Blaze threw his head back and roared.

FIFTEEN

Blaze frowned as he left the dungeon, closing the door behind him. Killing Stone hadn't brought him the pleasure he had thought it might. At least Phoebe and the other women were avenged. Yet his enjoyment of killing had dulled from what he remembered before he'd found his mate. His lust for her was far greater than it used to be for killing the enemy.

Martin Stone was the enemy. Anyone who tortured and murdered women for pleasure was a monster. Blaze had executed him without remorse.

With the destruction of civilization, the prison system was also destroyed. Early on, the Enclave banished lawbreakers. But that caused problems as the Enclave expanded or made them someone else's problem.

Blaze left Stone's house and walked crumbled sidewalks to check on the welfare of Sara Weeks, Stone's former housekeeper for Phoebe. He rapped his knuckles against the metal door frame and waited. A minute passed, and he knocked harder, as he could sense through his onboard scanner that people were in the house.

A woman in her forties with white-streaked blond hair opened the door wide. Behind her, a younger woman with a projectile rifle pointed it at him. "What do you want? Did Stone send you? I'm not giving that murdering bastard either of my girls. He can go to hell."

"I'm Ranger Blaze Savage, from the Civil Restoration Enclave of North America." He touched the badge he'd put back on his vest, a replica of the original Texas Rangers' badge. "I have been assigned to evaluate Old Texas in order to restore law and order. My female Phoebe Brooks asked me to check on your welfare."

"It's okay, Janie," Sara said. "Your female? Is she all right? What? Do you own her now?"

Blaze gave her a lopsided grin. "She is my wife. We belong to each other. Martin Stone was chasing her with four of his men, and I intervened. I've also come to inform you; your employer is dead."

"Well, I can't say I will miss him, but we will miss the things he gave us for working for him. He was a horrible man. He killed at least three women before he took up with Phoebe."

"Phoebe didn't have any friends in town when she met him, so she hadn't heard the rumors."

"She never suspected," Blaze agreed.

"One night, I forgot my bag and went back, and I saw his men carrying out the body of one of his women, Lucy. Somehow I knew she was dead." Sara opened the door and gestured for Blaze to enter. Her daughter put the rifle on safety and leaned it against the corner by the door. "Come in and sit for a few minutes." She led him across the foyer and to the left.

Blaze took the seat that she gestured. Sara and her daughter took seats on the couch, facing him.

"How is Phoebe? When I didn't see her for a few days, I started looking in every room of the house when he was out. The room where I found her was normally locked. I thought he had killed her when I found her, then she moaned."

"We hid her here four days," said Janie. "But she wouldn't stay any longer. She was afraid Stone would find out Mom freed her and do something bad to her."

"But she was too weak to saddle her horse, so I did it for her after the stable man left for the day," Sara said. "I didn't know if she was going to make it. Mr. Stone was livid when he found she was gone. He threatened everyone with dire consequences if he discovered who helped her."

"Did he find out?"

"No. When he asked me, I lied to his face," Sara said. "I'd gotten good at it over the years. He was an evil man, but he was also the most powerful man around. He called himself the Mayor, but he was more like a tyrant king."

"Is he really dead?" asked Janie.

"Yes... I...saw it happen." Blaze couldn't lie, but he saw no need to tell her he killed Stone. The Enclave wouldn't want a man like him interfering with restoring the community for law-abiding citizens. "Do you know anything about his other employees?"

"He had more than thirty. All their names and where they live are in his ledger," Sara told him.

"Yes, I saw the ledger on his desk while I was there," Blaze said.

"Do you know how he died?"

"He was beaten and stabbed in his own sex torture room."

"Good!" Sara said. "It's what he deserved. He killed three women before he hurt Phoebe. I don't doubt he would have killed her if I hadn't gotten her out of there."

"I know she was grateful for your help. Her body has healed; her mind will take a little longer."

"After Phoebe left, Stone tried to get me to let him court Janie. I told him she doesn't like men. It's not true; she just doesn't like him. She took care of Phoebe while I was working, so she saw what he did to her. Whoever killed him did this town a favor." Sara eyed Blaze, and he suspected she'd guessed that he killed Stone. She could hardly miss the collection of knives sheathed in his vest.

Blaze needed to do the cleanup resulting from Martin Stone's demise himself with no clean-up crew and no cleaning bots. First, he took out his comm-tablet to let Phoebe know he would be staying in Grafton for a few days. He used the tablet so she could see him while they talked. She wouldn't see him if he used his inner unit to make contact with her comm-tablet.

Phoebe took it well. She showed visible relief that Stone was dead and was happy that Sara was not punished for freeing her.

She told him excitedly about the progress they had made with her new garden using the sod breaker and bot-tiller. Blaze was a little disappointed that she was not more distressed about his delay in returning. But he wasn't worried about Javen moving in on his mate. She was Blaze's genetic mate, even though she didn't feel the connection as strongly as he did, but she hadn't waited nearly 100 years to find him.

Blaze's motivation for fighting the war against the Mesaarkans was the promise of finding her when it was over. There was a construct of her placed in his mind that resembled Phoebe closely. She came to him through the virtual reality program in his CPU. Her approximate physical structure was extrapolated from his DNA complement by the AI that programmed his cybernetics. The promise of her kept him alive when he began to falter, at times, wishing for death. Phoebe only had him in her life for a few weeks. While she didn't seem to be pining for him, she had seemed happy to see him on her com.

After chatting with Phoebe, Blaze went to the shed behind the house, looking for a pick and shovel to dig a grave for Stone. It would take hours for a regular man to dig a grave, but it was less than half an hour for a cyborg. Once he had buried Stone and cleaned up the blood in the dungeon, he dismantled it.

SIXTEEN

Blaze made Stone's house his temporary headquarters in Grafton. He spent three more days in the town, tracking down and questioning the former mayor's thugs to determine if they would be trouble makers. A few of them were defiant, but most of them just worked for him so they could eat regularly.

Most of them didn't really like him because they had been oppressed if they made mistakes. Only Stone's top man Clade wasn't willing to take the offer of property and a new start. The others seemed to think Clade was planning to terminate Stone and take over the rule of Grafton.

"Who the hell are you to come here and tell us how to run our town? Martin Stone took care of these people. Where the hell is he anyway?"

"Gone," Blaze told him. "Did you know he tortured and killed three women?"

"Three? I only knew about one, and Mr. Stone said it was an accident. Tom and Pete buried her."

"According to my source, she was the last of three."

"Sara. If… and I mean if, then he took care of them himself," Clade said.

"She wasn't lying. There were no physical indications."

"How the hell do you know that?"

"I am a cyborg. I have integrated scanners."

"I don't care what you are. What gives you the right to come into our town and take over?"

"The Federation and the Enclave. The war with the Mesaarkans set Earth back 3.673 centuries."

"Why here?"

"Phoebe."

"The Boss's woman?"

"No, *my* wife," Blaze said in no uncertain terms. "Your boss damaged her. That's why she was running away. Females are not property. The world population was decimated by the bombings. Females have been enslaved and abused by overlords and gangers in the ruined cities. You will either comply with the laws which once governed this continent or leave Enclave territory."

132

"So, you can take over?"

"I am an enforcer. We cyborgs, fought for the promise of a genetic mate to breed and make offspring. Communities must be safe for families. Strong families build strong communities," Blaze explained. "If you continue your objective to control this town, I will stop you. You can either go to prison offworld, or you can go east to Farringay and become a ganger for Alexander Berke."

"What if I don't want to leave?"

"Then you follow the laws that will govern this town."

Clade gave him a mutinous look. "I want Stone's place, or are you claiming it?"

"I am not. My home is in a remote location. There will be cyborg protectors assigned to this town under my command. Do not make the mistake of resuming Stone's agenda when I leave. If you do, I will come for you."

Phoebe had been busy the first day; Blaze was gone, so she hadn't missed him until she went to bed alone. She could hardly believe he had only been a part of her life for a couple weeks. As she lay in bed alone, she found herself pining for him, aching for his kisses and to have his big body on her and in her, claiming her with every thrust.

The cyborg Javen helped to section off the garden plot and set the bot-tiller to prepare the soil for planting. However, he was not much of a conversationalist. He rarely spoke at all unless she asked him a direct question.

Was this what being Blaze's mate would be like? Alone for days on end while he went on his missions. Why hadn't she felt this loneliness all the months she spent at her home by herself?

Then she answered her own question. It was a relief to be alone after the abuse she suffered from Martin Stone. When Blaze told her he would be gone a few more days, she hid her disappointment, smiling when she felt like crying.

Phoebe was lying in bed trying to sleep in the darkened cabin when a noise drew her attention. She sat up in bed, reaching for the laser pistol under her pillow. A man stood at the end of her bed, silhouetted in the moonlight from the skylight overhead.

She started to raise the pistol, but when she saw him pull off his shirt, she knew the only danger was mind-blowing sex with her mate. "Blaze!" she exclaimed happily.

She jumped out of bed and lunged at him. He caught her in his arms and lifted her up, so they were face to face. Phoebe wrapped her legs around his hips, murmuring, "I missed you so much!"

"My sweet female," he uttered just before his mouth fused with hers. They both moaned as their tongues swirled around each other.

Blaze hugged her tight against his chest, and she relished the pressure against her breasts. While they kissed, she hugged him with her legs and rubbed her mons against his abdomen. The nights seemed so much longer without him.

Still kissing her, Blaze rolled them onto the bed, with her on her back beneath him.

"Now, Blaze," she whispered when he freed her lips. "I need you now."

"Yes, I scent your arousal," he whispered back.

"And I feel your hardness... Put it inside me."

He shifted over her and slid into her, eliciting a vocal sigh of approval from her. He kissed her again, reached between them, caught her taut nipples between his thumbs and forefingers, and pinched them. As she hummed her pleasure, he withdrew and thrust into her. He flexed his hips to put pressure on her clit.

Phoebe clung to his back, pressing her finger tips into his flesh. He seemed to know exactly what she needed, and he made it his mission to give it to her.

When he ended the kiss, she looked up into his eyes as he watched her face intently. He pinched her nipples to the verge of pain and pleasure. At the same time, he pulled almost out of her and rammed his cock into her hard and deep. She gasped her pleasure and murmured his name. As her body tensed with the coiling low in her belly, Blaze took her a little faster until she shook him with the first contractions of her orgasm.

She adored that he teased her through it until it played out, though she knew they were far from finished. She hugged him tenderly.

"It seemed like you were gone forever."

"Four days, ten hours, forty-seven minutes, and nineteen seconds."

"Ah Blaze. It seemed so much longer."

"It did for me, too," he said and kissed her, making his cock pulse inside her.

"More," she encouraged, caressing his face.

Blaze turned his head and kissed her palm, moving his hand up to caress her face and play with her hair. He claimed her lips in a passionate, tongue tangoing kiss and started pumping in and out of her.

Phoebe adored the strength of his solid, muscular body, relishing the power of his hard, deep thrusts as he took her. She reveled in the feel of his rigid cock caressing her inner walls and that sweet spot. When Blaze was breeding her, she was in the moment with him as their bodies slammed together in their erotic rhythm. He gave as much as he took while she keened and crooned her pleasure as they soared toward ecstasy together.

Phoebe cried out as Blaze came, pouring his seed inside her, and she came with him in a mutual climax that played out each in response to the other. She could see the pleasure in his eyes as he throbbed inside her, and she tightened her sheath around his cock. Seeing his happiness and his devotion in his eyes took her outside herself as she began to sense the special connection, she shared with him.

Was this love? Giving each other what they needed. The sex was only part of it, as fantastic as it was. Before Blaze, her limited experience with men was worse than lackluster.

Had Blaze not come on the scene when he did, Martin Stone and his men would have caught her. She would probably be dead. Martin didn't want her back because he loved her; he wanted her back so he could finish killing her.

When she looked into Blaze's eyes, she saw a man with a pure heart. He wanted to love and be loved. Breed and make offspring. To have a family with her.

She wondered what it was like to have a real family. Phoebe had been an only child. Her father had left when she was almost too young to remember him. Her mother never believed he just left them. She said he must be dead, or he would have come back. Phoebe didn't know if it were true or just what her mother wanted to believe.

Yet, the few memories she had of her father were good ones. He seemed to love her mother and her. So, maybe her mother was right that he never came back because he couldn't.

SEVENTEEN

Phoebe thought it was a dream. She was wrapped in Blaze's arms, and he was caressing her in deliciously arousing places. He was kneading her breasts and plucking at her nipples, then one hand slid down her belly between her legs. A finger slid over her clit and into her wet channel and back to her clit. He felt so good. If he kept doing what he was doing, she would orgasm.

She made a purring sound in her throat, giving herself into the enjoyment of his intimate caresses. As she felt the climax building low in her belly, she registered his erection pressing against her bottom. It seemed almost sudden when the orgasm rippled through her body, and she opened her eyes to find Blaze wrapped around her.

She murmured his name and gasped as another contraction rippled through her. Nuzzling her neck where it met her shoulder, he said, "you feel good."

"Ooh, yeah, I do," she said, ending her sentence with a sigh.

He turned her on her back, putting his leg between hers. "Want me to make you feel even better?" He asked with a sexy grin that was nearly impossible to resist, though resisting was the last thing on her mind as he leaned in and took her taut nipple in his mouth and sucked on it.

A surge of pleasure shot straight to her clit. By the time he finished sucking on it, her mind had shifted to how much she wanted him to sink that long, hard cock of his deep into her core. He moved, so his hips were between her legs.

Phoebe was all in by then, caressing his head, shoulders, and back as he savored her body, drawing sighs and moans of pleasure. He moved down her body, slowly drawing closer to her mons. She began to pant as he parted her nether lips and pressed his lips to her clit, tonguing and sucking it.

The pleasure was sweet torment, but he backed off before she came to feast on the juices in her channel. Phoebe moaned and cried out when he turned his attention back to her sensitive bud until she screamed in orgasm, trying to buck her hips as the force of it seized her body.

Blaze turned her over, put her on her hands and knees, and slid his cock into her from behind. She clamped down on it immediately, still in the throes of her intense orgasm. Phoebe wailed his name as his entry increased her satisfaction. He thrust in and out of her slowly at first, increasing speed. Soon he was pounding into her as if he could never get enough of her.

He gave her two more orgasms before the grand finale when he poured his essence into her and shouted his enjoyment. He leaned over, still inside her, and kissed the back of her neck while kneading her breasts.

"Mm," she hummed. "So... Good..." She balanced on the one hand and caressed his hand as he enjoyed her breasts.

When they finally separated, Blaze scooped her up and carried her into the shower. There he washed her tenderly and made love to her again, slowly and sweetly.

After they finished their shower and dressed, they went to the kitchen, and Blaze set out a breakfast of meal bars and fruit juice. He sat beside her at their small dining table and took a sip of his juice while Phoebe opened her meal bar.

"If we had a way to cook and some cookware, I could prepare regular food," she said.

"There were too many variables for me to accurately predict finding my mate, so I didn't foresee a need for a food processor," Blaze said.

"If we get something to cook, we could dig a firepit outside. I had a good old cast iron cooking pot and a frying pan. They would still be in the ruins of my house. Could we go back sometime and look through the wreckage?"

"As you wish, my mate. I promised your friend Sara that I would take you to see her. We could make a detour on the way back,"

"What happened to Martin?" she asked. The mention of Sara sparked the memory of how they became friends.

Blaze met her gaze, hesitating, knowing he could only tell her the truth or tell her nothing. "I killed him."

Sara looked away for a few seconds, processing his admission, then back at him again. "Good. I hope you made him suffer."

"I did." He didn't elaborate.

"Will you get in trouble for killing him?"

"Not with Cyborg Command or the Enclave," he said. "Only three of his employees refused to comply with the rules of the Enclave. I banished them."

"So, what happens to the town now?"

"The Enclave is sending a team of advisors who will bring comm-tablets and help them organize a democratic government to run the town. An engineer with a construction crew will restore utilities to the homes, and protectors will be assigned to live in the town to enforce the law."

"I don't understand why you started your mission with Grafton? There used to be hundreds of Texas towns from the old history books my mom taught me from. At least a dozen closer to here than Grafton."

"I was just doing a flyover and saw you being chased by Stone and his men. I was duty-bound to investigate. His explanation was not logical. A simple misunderstanding does not normally make a female run all out to get away."

"You got that right. Now that I think back, I am lucky they didn't shoot Brandy and Sherry before we got back to rescue them," Phoebe said, the hint of tears welling in her eyes. "It makes me so fucking mad that they killed those sweet little goats and my chickens who never hurt anyone."

Blaze took her hand and pulled her onto his lap. "I am sorry I didn't get there in time to stop that. But weren't they used for their meat?"

"No," she sniffed as tears ran down her cheeks. "I couldn't kill them. I milked them and made cheese and soap. I cried every time I killed a chicken for food. Mostly, I just took their eggs."

"Then you ate mostly vegetables?"

"Yes, we saved seeds every year and planted them the next year... I did the same after Mama died until Martin. I gave my livestock to a neighbor, and they gave me some back when I went back home."

Blaze kissed her tears away, not knowing what to say that would ease her sorrow. She wept softly for a couple of minutes. After he kissed her tears away, he kissed her lips tenderly. It was the only way he could think to let her know he cared how she felt.

Phoebe kissed him back, seeming to understand his kisses were not meant to be a prelude to sex. Even so, they were still rousing. She finally ended yet another kiss and just hugged Blaze resting her head on his shoulder. "I could kiss you all day," she murmured. "But that won't get the animals fed. We've already made them wait for hours past when I usually feed them."

She slid off his lap and stood, giving him a rueful look. Blaze nodded slightly, as though he understood she had responsibilities, too. He followed her outside.

"I was surprised that Javen even brought another large bag of dog food with the supplies you ordered. Brandy seems to like it," Phoebe told him as they walked to the shed.

"The Enclave has restored production of many essentials in the New Chicago area. It's not the metropolis as it once was before the bombings. Now it's a large town surrounded by homesteads where suburbs once were," Blaze said. "They are hoping to extend the development throughout North America west of the Appalachians."

The horse and goats grazing in the makeshift pasture followed them in because they already learned that's where they got fed their supplemental food. Food and water receptacles had been installed in the shed for all the animals.

"How come only west of the Appalachians?"

"Because the Federation commanded it. Commander Dark said it has to do with an overlord who has more powerful friends than the Enclave. We could fight the overlord and the gangers, but we can't fight the Federation."

They stood watching the animals munch their food. "The chicks are growing fast, pretty soon they will need nests because they will start laying eggs in a few weeks."

"No problem. I will have Javen bring a kit to assemble one. He will be glad to have something to do."

"But how are you getting all this stuff for the animals and the garden? Don't you have to pay for it? We hadn't had money around here since way before I was born... I mean, we had some, but it wasn't worth anything."

"It will change as the government and manufacturing are restored. But we don't have to worry about paying for necessities. I have accumulated ninety years of combat pay to provide whatever we need."

"That's probably good because as often as we are breeding, we will probably make me pregnant sooner or later." Phoebe blushed as he gave her a blatantly sexual look that made her core clench. How could she want him this much again already? She felt like she was in heat, almost continually in his presence.

The sexy grin he gave her left no doubt that he already scented her arousal. It was not that she didn't adore fucking him. That was awesome, but in truth, she only knew him for a day when she made the commitment to being his mate for life. She frowned, and she saw Blaze's smile fade.

"You do not wish to breed?"

EIGHTEEN

Phoebe went to him and slid her arms around his waist, looking up to meet his gaze. "I do, but not right now. I already know your body way better than I know *you*. This is almost as new for me as it is for you. The attraction between us is like nothing I ever felt for anyone else. I never even heard of cyborgs before you came here."

"Because we were just in experimental stages before the war, and it was a top-secret military project. By the time it was made public, mass communications on Earth were destroyed." He paused, putting his arms around her and rubbing her back. "Phoebe, you can ask me anything you want to know about me, and I will tell you honestly."

"And I believe that. It's just that everything happened so fast... My head and my heart haven't caught up with my sex parts."

"You are everything I thought you would be; you were programmed into my genes. I have always known you... Always loved you."

"It's not like that for me. I feel like you cast some sort of spell over me that every time I am near you, I want you to rip off my clothes and fuck me." She frowned. "That's not me. I feel like I am out of control."

Blaze caressed her cheek as she looked up at him earnestly. "You are reacting as you were meant to. It's not a spell; it's physiology. You recognized me as your mate on a purely physical level. I was sensitized to your scent, and I expected to react to you when I met you."

"So, you had a head start on this thing between us."

"Yes," he said. He framed Phoebe's face in his hands and kissed her, knowing she was aware of his erection pressed against her belly. "But it's more than just sexual attraction. I can see in your eyes that you care for me... And in the way, you breed with me."

"I do like you... Very much," she admitted. "I can't even imagine breeding with anyone but you."

"I believe you."

"Why do you think they made you like this so you could only have one mate?"

"They didn't want us spreading our genes around in the general population. We were kept in stasis, where they brainwashed us in our virtual lives. You were there in mine. But when I was awakened, you were a memory. I believed I would find you again after the war." He paused, looking as though he'd conjured a memory that was too painful to speak of.

Phoebe didn't know what to say, so she just waited for him to go on.

"I took a bad hit on a dangerous mission, and the Commander over our unit chose to leave me behind rather than risk any more men to carry me out. He figured I was as good as dead. I was still alive when the Mesaarkans found me. They made me wish for death, tortured me for information I didn't have. I think they knew that eventually; they just wanted to make me suffer. But the promise of you kept me from giving up."

"Oh, Blaze. That's terrible... that they tortured you." She reached up to caress his cheek.

"By the time the war was over, I wasn't ready to look for you. I went to Phantom, the cyborg colony, to decompress. Then I got a call from Commander Dark for this job. He has a newbie collecting DNA for a database to match cyborgs with their females or their males. I hoped they would eventually find my match."

151

"I think maybe fate stepped in and brought you to me when I most needed you." Phoebe hugged him. "When is your next mission?"

"It's ongoing, but I won't be going out again for two more days. I want more time with you."

"Can we go check the ruins of my house for salvageable cookware?"

"If that is what you wish. I don't want you upset because of what Stone did to your home and your animals."

"I am upset about it, but I knew I could never live there as long as Martin was alive. He was obsessed. He would have killed me if you hadn't stopped him. Now, I just hope we can salvage something from my house," she said. "I like it here."

"The Enclave found it for me. I just told them I wanted a remote location with its own power source in my territory."

"If we make children, we will need more space, though."

"They are making prefab sections of aerated concrete up north that can be assembled in days. We can look at what's available on our tablets," he said with an endearing look on his face. "I am happy you're thinking about making children with me."

Phoebe chuckled. "Well, since birth control for women these days is not breeding, it's something we should think about."

"My nanites must be programmed to produce sperm for you to become pregnant. So, you must tell me when you are ready to make offspring." They were still standing in the yard, talking with their arms around each other in the sunshine.

"When were you going to tell me that," she asked, curious.

"Whenever we discussed making offspring, as we are now. I truly want to make a family with you, but for now, I think we need time to bond before we make offspring." He leaned down and kissed her lips with restrained passion.

"Because you want me all to yourself?" she asked with a smile.

Blaze smiled back at her. "We need that right now, I think."

Phoebe nodded. "I never had a formal education, but I read most of the books we had, including textbooks. Somewhere, I read, couples should give themselves time together before having children."

"Let's walk," Blaze suggested, taking her hand. "We've not even covered half the ground on this property. Some places are too overgrown. The property was left unattended for 99 years."

"What are we going to do with all of this land? It would be good to ride Sherry and explore, but some of it is pretty thick with underbrush."

"I think we should keep it mostly wild with plain dirt trails for walking or riding your horse. Since she is no longer your only means of transport, you only need to ride for pleasure."

"How do you feel about getting another horse so we can ride together?" Phoebe asked, hopefully.

"I'd need a strong horse because I am much heavier than a natural-born man of my size and build."

"Traveling for your job, you might locate a stronger breed of horse," she said. "People around here use horses for everything. Farmers use draft horses if they can. They are big and gentle, probably strong enough to carry you."

"I'll look around for one in my travels. Meanwhile, I can easily keep up with you on foot."

"It wouldn't be the same. If you are walking, I would rather walk with you."

The land surrounding the cabin was thickly wooded in some areas where others were covered in a mixture of tall grasses, which they tramped down as they walked.

"Cutting some real paths through the tall grasses will make it easier to walk."

"Better to see snakes before you step on them too. I've seen copperheads and rattlers from time to time, but they don't bother you if you keep your distance," said Phoebe.

"Copperheads and rattlers are poisonous," Blaze said with a hint of concern.

"That's why a path is a good idea, with grass this tall. There's plenty of room for livestock, though we don't need to raise any. I wouldn't want the little goats out here alone, even with Brandy. We had wolf sightings around my place. They would be easy pickings for a wolf." She fell silent as she flashed back on the little goat bodies in front of her barn.

Blaze stopped and turned to face her, sensing a change in her breathing and heartbeat. Her eyes were brimming with tears. "You still mourn the goats Stone's thugs killed."

"They were almost as helpless as kittens. It makes me so mad."

"I'm sorry we didn't get back in time to stop them. I believe they burned your house and killed your animals on their way to catch you. Whichever men killed them; Martin ordered it."

Blaze rested his hands on her shoulders, casually massaging them lightly. "And he is dead."

Phoebe wiped the tears from her eyes with her fingers and sighed. "I will just have to find some more to rebuild the herd... A *small* herd."

"We will get security drones to guard them against all predators. Programed properly, they will keep predators away from them by non-lethal means. The Enclave has regulations about preserving indigenous species that have repopulated since the human population was decimated by the bombings."

"That all happened before I was born. But I saw vids on the tablet about the bombings. It must have been terrible."

"That was before my time, too. Most of the cities are still in ruins. I saw that first hand."

"Are they going to rebuild the cities?"

"Only some of the strategically located ones. The population numbers don't warrant rebuilding them all. We're going to relocate the people living in the ruins."

"That's not part of your job, is it?"

"No, I'm here to make sure the towns are run by the residents and not crime bosses like Stone."

"By yourself?"

"I'm just doing recon. I will eventually be supervising protectors who will maintain order."

"Who protects you?"

"I do."

NINETEEN

They spent the two days Blaze was home, doing everything together when they were not making love. He contacted some of his cyborg friends to find some little goats for Phoebe and a big horse for himself. As far as he was concerned, they were small things he could do for his female to help her get past the damage Stone had done to her.

Killing her animals was especially cruel because they weren't just livestock to her. They were companions... pets. Making cheese and soap from their milk was no longer a necessity, but she enjoyed doing it. She'd spent her life as a homesteader, and she wanted to continue in her life with Blaze. That was highly encouraged by the Enclave.

Instead of the factory farms of the past, vat farms kept small herds and flocks to harvest cells for cultured meat instead of raising and killing large herds and flocks. It was better for the environment using a technique like breeding cyborgs, but far less complex. Cultured meat was grown from muscle cells instead of embryos.

Two glorious days one on one with Phoebe was not enough. But he'd agreed to do a job, and cyborg honor wouldn't allow him to renege on his duty. Nor his commitment to his female. Those were the two things that made cyborgs sought after as mates in the Enclave's eastern territories. Cyborg teams were collecting DNA from women to match with cyborgs looking for genetic mates.

They determined from old Enclave records that the cyborgs produced in both the Chicago and the Machu Pichu facilities were genetically programmed to accept only one genetic mate. The creators were required to make them that way to limit the possibility they would breed with normal females in the general population.

Those people were dead and gone. Now the cyborg medics had studied the criteria for finding those mates via DNA matching. The match rate was only limited by the database size, but it was expanding nearly every day. Blaze continued to marvel that he had found his mate by pure luck since their promise of a mate and family was an empty one. The lie was to motivate them to fight for the Federation.

The odds were rigged against them. So, they came up with a work-around. As he pulled communities into the fold, Blaze would promote the mate project to help fellow cyborgs find their mates.

Blaze wasn't deluding himself that Phoebe fell instantly in love with him just because they had great sex. Stone had done a lot of damage to her psyche with his cruelty. Yet when they did have sex, he believed their bonds were strengthening. Blaze would never find tying and torturing someone sexually arousing. That's what the Mesaarkans had done to him; chained him and inflicted pain until he wished for death to make it end. Not once did he feel aroused. All he felt was agonizing pain.

As far as he was concerned, Stone was a blight on humanity. Blaze had ended many beings in his years at war, none more deserving than Stone. His foremost reason was that Stone hurt Phoebe. He could feel no remorse for killing anyone who harmed his mate.

On the other hand, it brought him great pleasure to do small things to make her happy.

"I wish I could go with you," Phoebe said plaintively as they watched the two goats and the horse grazing in the pasture while waiting for her bodyguard to arrive.

"It might be dangerous, depending on what I find when I get to some of these places. The crime bosses that run some of these towns will be less than cordial on my arrival," he told her. "I would worry more about keeping you safe than doing my job."

"I know," she murmured, putting her arms around his waist and resting her cheek against his chest. "The days seem a hundred hours long when you're away."

"Then you'll be extra glad to see me when I get back." But when she looked up at him as she was doing then, it made him want to do everything to he could to take that sadness from her eyes and her heart.

"How long will you be gone this time?"

"Three to four days. Having you here where you are safe will let me do my job. Before I come back, I will stop at your house and see if there is anything to salvage."

"But I thought we were going together."

"It will only upset you again. I want to do some cleanup before I take you there again. Besides, Javen is bringing you a surprise from me. A couple, actually."

Blaze chucked gently under her chin and lowered his mouth to hers in a tender kiss. "I will pull out whatever I find in the ashes and set it aside. Then I will take you there to sort through it."

"All right," she sighed. "This is all your fault, you know. I spent months alone at my farmstead, working contentedly on my projects. Then you showed up in my life and made me relish your company. Now you are going away to your job. I worry that something bad will happen, and you won't come back."

"I was a combat specialist in the cyborg rangers for 90 years. Ordinary projectile weapons can barely penetrate my skin. Plus, I have armor and superior weapons. Farringay is the only place where modern weapons are available. The probability of such weapons this far west is 2.0902 percent. And the Enclave has a treaty with Farringay that does not allow them to trade west of the Appalachians."

A subtle whining sound drew their attention to the sky as a large transport flyer was making a landing approach. Blaze reluctantly released Phoebe from his embrace. As soon as the craft touched down and settled, they walked across the front yard to meet Javen.

Although his land was quite a distance from the nearest neighbors, Blaze wouldn't consider leaving his mate unprotected in his absence. Less than a minute after landing, Javen was descending the flyer's exit ramp with a small goat under each arm.

"Oh," Phoebe squealed. "They are so precious!"

Javen nodded in greeting, handing one goat off to Blaze and one to Phoebe. "There're more." He went back into the vehicle and came back with two more babies under his arms. "They are all weaned, and this one is a male unrelated to the others. I brought a shed kit and more fencing for your nanny and the kids. Plus, the bot-sod cutter to make the path through your grasslands."

"Blaze, what a great surprise. I love them," she smiled up at him while cuddling the little goat kid in her arms. We can put them in the shed while we get their pen set up. Separating them from Sherry, will keep them from getting trampled accidentally."

"Then I have to go," Blaze said.

Phoebe met his gaze and nodded resolutely. "Did you tell Javen the route for the path we are building?"

"I'll leave that up to you. I transmitted the coordinates of our boundaries on the property.

There is plenty of room to make a few trails," Blaze told her as they carried the goats to the shed.

Once they were safely installed, Javen returned to the transport to unload the machine. Blaze swept Phoebe into his arms, lifting her off the ground, so they were chest to chest, and kissed her long and slow. He wanted to carry her back into the house and breed with her instead of leaving her, but he knew his job was vital to bring the western states into the Enclave.

When he finally lifted his lips from hers, his cock was hard and making his pants feel tight in the crotch. He could scent her arousal as he let her slide down his front until her feet touched the ground again. Kissing her like that was probably a bad idea, as it made leaving her harder than it was already.

She was a bit disoriented as she looked up at him with a vague smile. "I'll keep that thought until you come back."

Blaze turned resolutely and strode out of the shed without looking back. If he saw that yearning in her eyes again, he wasn't sure he could make himself leave her.

Taking down the tyrannical bosses and their underlings was the only way to make these communities safe for families raising children. Now that he had his female to breed, his job's importance took on new relevance in his own life, he reminded himself as he climbed on his sky cycle.

TWENTY

Blaze's first stop was a village named Sycamore, fifty miles north of his ranch hideaway. It appeared he'd crossed a line between the lush green surrounding his home and more arid land. Lawns were patchy, and the flora was more arid hardy than his region.

As he glided over the town, he could hear gunfire, multiple guns firing. He increased his altitude and flew the craft in the direction of the shooting. He soon located the gunfire sources, but he had no way to contact either side without going down there himself. Blaze flew past them and found a place to land and secure his sky cycle.

He pulled out his ion rifle, shouldered it, and set his blaster to stun. Activating his full body armor, he waited for it to cover him. The new smart armor expanded over his body, leaving a gun belt, ion rifle, and weapons vest on the outside.

Blaze didn't feel like getting pelted with bullets just to prove he was almost impervious. They would still hurt, and a head shot with large caliber ammo could give him a concussion and knock him out. He walked down the middle of the street and stopped between the two buildings they were shooting from.

"Cease fire! Cease fire!" he shouted, though it was unnecessary because they stopped firing from both sides. He was sure they had never seen a cyborg in full battle regalia before, and none with a silver replica of a Texas Ranger badge embossed in the armor. They probably didn't even know the war had been over for several years.

"I am Federation Ranger Captain Blaze Savage. The Mesaarkan war is over, and I am here to re-establish law and order in the former state of Texas. You will put down your weapons. I will listen to both sides of this altercation and determine how the law should be applied."

Blaze went to the building, where he scanned only two men inside. The old storefront was boarded up with a freehand painted sign that said 'Sheriff.' Blaze receded his armor's helmet so the men could see his face.

"Ranger, they came to my house three days ago and took my daughter while I was out working the fields. They took other girls, too.

My boy and I came to town to find them, and they started shooting at us as we rode in."

"How do you know they took your daughter?" Blaze asked the older man.

"Mariah Jonas saw my Carrie with them. She said my girl looked like she didn't want to be with them. I think they're trying to get rid of Ned and me, so they don't have to answer for it. The last sheriff we had was killed more than a month ago, and the new one is missing. No one else will take the job."

"Someone will now. I've been sent to assess the need town by town and make recommendations to command. They will send cyborg protectors," Blaze said. "What are your names?"

"As I said, this is my son, Ned Brown, and I am Lucas Brown."

"Do you know who is shooting at you?"

"Don't know their names; I've seen them in the village a few times. They are new in town, only here a month," Lucas said. "We were never introduced. Ned's friend Maria told him they were staying in that old storefront across the street. We just came to talk, and they started shooting."

"Nobody should be shooting in a neighborhood like this. It's too easy for a shot to ricochet and hit an innocent," Blaze admonished.

"We only meant to defend ourselves," said Lucas. "We only shot at where the shots were coming from."

"How old is your daughter?"

"She is nineteen."

"Please wait here, and I will talk to the people across the street." Blaze extended his helmet over his head and face, striding out of the office and across the street. As he moved, he appreciated that the new smart armor was thin and light, allowing a more natural gait.

As he expected, the three men in the storefront across the street met him with guns pointed at his head. "Put down your guns, or I will take them from you," Blaze ordered. None of them missed the embossed circled ranger star on his left chest as it was large enough to see from a distance.

They holstered their guns, which were semiautomatic replicas of old-style western six guns. "Mr. Brown said you took his daughter along with some other girls," Blaze asked, retracting the helmet.

"We didn't kidnap her. She came of her own free will."

"Where is she now?" Blaze demanded.

"She's at our farmhouse about fifteen miles from town."

"Your names, please."

"I'm Dan, that's Joe, and he is Fred. We're cousins, and we live on the farm."

"Are there any other girls on the farm?"

"Ellie Baker and Hollie Peters. We just came to town for supplies and stopped to see a friend, but he's not here."

"Who started the shooting?"

"I fired a warning shot. They went into the sheriff's office and started shooting at us."

He was lying, but Blaze saw no reason to call him on it. The only truth that mattered was whether Brown's daughter left of her own accord and if she was safe.

"While you have the right to bear arms, you do not have the right to fire one in a residential area unless you are defending your life. You should hope no innocent was hurt in the crossfire or by a stray bullet," Blaze warned. "What are the coordinates of this farmhouse where Brown's daughter is."

"Huh?" Dan said with a puzzled frown.

"Location... I need to speak with Carrie Brown to make sure she safe and there of her own free will."

"Take this road out of town going that way." Dan pointed. "Our house is the third on the right. It's a white house with no other houses around it."

Blaze started to leave, then he decided the townspeople would be safer if he disarmed these three men and the Browns before he left. Before they realized his intention, he had taken their guns and was running across the street to take the Browns' guns as well. He zip-tied them together and carried them as he ran to his sky cycle.

Chucking them into the cargo compartment, there was just enough room for him to close it. He let his armor retract into the plate at the small of his back as he jumped on his sky cycle and set it in motion gliding over the road at 85mph.

The man named Dan was lying about the gunfight, and he was lying about Brown's daughter. Minutes later, with the house in sight, he increased the altitude. As he hovered above the house, he discovered a hovercraft parked in front of it. A woman was screaming and struggling between two men who were trying to drag her to the craft.

Blaze quickly landed the cycle beside the craft, jumped off, and grabbed each man by the throat. "Let her go!"

Each man let go of her arm and tried to pry Blaze's hands from their throats. The girl sat down on the porch step of the house; her hands tied behind her back.

Blaze only held the other two men until they passed out and lowered them to the ground. He pulled more zip ties from his utility belt and tied the men's hands behind their backs as they lay unconscious. He double-checked to make sure he had inflicted no permanent damage to them.

With them secured, he turned to the young woman. "Are you all right?"

He squatted down beside her and cut the rope that bound her hands.

"I'm fine," she said, fighting back tears. "Two other girls are in that car. They were taking us east to sell us to a brothel."

"Are you Carrie Brown?" Blaze asked.

"Yes. I am such a fool. They tricked us, invited us to a party. We got there, and there was not much to drink and hardly any food. Then they were going to town for supplies, and these guys showed up while Dan and his friends were gone. It was all arranged for these two to kidnap us."

Blaze went to the craft and found the other two girls bound and gagged on the floor inside. He untied them and ungagged them.

"Who are you? What's happening?"

He gave them the requested information as he did a quick scan to confirm that they were uninjured and took a DNA profile to add to the cyborg matching databank. He would explain it to them on the trip back into town.

"Daddy is going to kill me," Carrie said when the other two girls emerged from the hovercar.

"He might be angry, but when I spoke to him, he was very concerned that these men had stolen or hurt you," said Blaze. "I believe he will be relieved that you are unharmed."

Blaze bound the men's ankles together and picked them both up by the waistbands of their pants, and stowed them in their craft on the floor where the girls had been.

173

"Carrie, if you and your friends…"

"Beth and Julie," Carrie filled in for him.

"Beth and Julie will climb into the craft; I will take you all back to town. These men and their friends will answer for their crimes."

Blaze paused to program his sky cycle to return to the coordinates where he had secured it. Climbing into the driver's seat of the antiquated hovercraft, he linked to the onboard computer and programmed it to take them back to town.

TWENTY-ONE

While driving the lumbering old craft back to Sycamore, Blaze contacted cyborg control in New Chicago to send transport for the prisoners and two protectors to the town. Arriving at the sheriff's office, he parked the vehicle in front of it. A crowd had gathered.

Blaze climbed out first, and people opened a path to the Sheriff's office. When Carrie stepped out, her father ran to hug her. The parents of the other two young women came forward to embrace their daughters. As Blaze looked at the building across the street, he noted it was now empty.

"Are you going to be the new sheriff," asked one of them.

"There will be Protectors assigned to your town to start," said Blaze. To the rest of the bystanders, he said, "How is your town governed? I need to meet with those people in charge."

"I'm the Mayor," a man raised his hand, and we have a council of seven people who run things."

"I need to meet with you to explain what has happened since the end of the Mesaarkan war."

"I think we are all here now. Everyone came running when the gunfire stopped," said the mayor.

"Those three fellas who took the girls ran off as soon as you left, Ranger," said Ned Brown.

"I will find them again," Blaze assured him. "They are kidnappers working for the Eastern Overlords. The overlords are paying bounties on attractive young females to staff their brothels. It is apparently substantial for their *gangers* to come west to kidnap and transport them East."

"Ranger, are there more like you where you come from?" asked Beth's mother. "We just don't have enough men to go around. These kidnappers said they came here to find a wives and settle down."

"There is a program for females to sign up to be tested for a cyborg mate. My kind has been made to mate only with a female with a specific DNA profile."

"I don't know what that is," said the woman.

"It's what determines your physical traits. Only a genetic mate can produce children with a cyborg. Females can register for a scan, and our technician will search for a match. That is the most efficient way to find a cyborg mate."

"What if she doesn't want children?"

"Cyborgs are programmed to desire children. I don't know of any cyborgs who have non-genetic mates."

"How about you. Ranger? Do you have a mate?"

"I do," he replied.

"Do cyborgs get married? We want our girls to have husbands, not just mates."

"We have a mating vow to pledge our lives to each other. It means the same thing to us."

There were more questions about getting cyborg mates for their daughters than returning their community to law and order. They followed those questions with more questions about how cyborgs differed from natural men, spawning more questions.

"I understand you are all curious about my kind, but there will be others who come after me who are more versed in these matters," Blaze finally said. "While these lawbreakers are waiting for transport, I need to meet with your mayor and council about the law enforcement needs in your community. That is my part of the job. Once your village is secure, Enclave representatives will come to enlist for the cyborg mating program, restore communications and power to your homes, and inform you about the state of Earth, the Federation, and the new Earth Government."

He paused, looking over the people surrounding him. "Does anyone believe this town is in danger or that you are in danger?"

"I want to know what happened to my husband. He was the sheriff. One day he went to work, but he never came home, and it's been a week."

She was an attractive young woman, though plainly dressed, with a toddler in her arms. "The new protectors will look into that for you. They will want to talk to you soon after I brief them on the situation here."

"When? He's already been gone three days. He could be somewhere out there hurt… Or he could be dead…" She started to cry.

Blaze frowned and sighed. She was right. Investigating what happened to the sheriff shouldn't wait. It could make the difference between finding him alive rather than dead.

"Where was he going when he left?" Blaze asked.

"He was going out to find out what happened to these three girls. Now you brought them back; where is he?"

"What is your name?"

"Millie Robins. My husband is Fred," she said.

"Did he say where he was going to start looking?"

"He was going to head west out of town. He was riding his brown and white pinto."

"All right. I'll head out that way after I talk to the Mayor and town council."

"But it will be getting dark pretty soon."

"Ma'am, I can see just fine in the dark. I'm a cyborg."

Blaze spent just over an hour explaining the function of the Enclave. Although the Enclave had annexed the territory in parts of the former USA, Canada and Mexico, the towns and villages would maintain their autonomy. However, the criminal code would be enforced uniformly throughout the annexed territories.

The Cyborg Rangers would provide law enforcement in the former western states until Protectors could be assigned to the communities. The rangers would then serve as supervisors within their territories. Their most prominent and urgent mission was to remove the overlords and crime bosses who had taken over the towns.

Blaze summoned his sky cycle and headed west out of town to see if he could find the sheriff. As Millie Robins said, it was dark by the time he left. About ten miles out of town, he spotted the paint horse still saddled but without its rider.

Circling around a few times in a widening route, he found a man lying in the grass in a small grove of trees. His heat signature told Blaze the man was alive and about two miles from the horse.

Blaze landed a few yards away and walked toward the man on the ground.

"Hold it right there." The man sat up, pointing a pistol at him.

"You Fred Robins?"

"Who's asking?"

"Ranger Blaze Savage. Are you Robins?"

"Yeah, my horse spooked and ran me into a low hanging branch. He took off, and I've been dizzy and nauseated… Don't know how long I was out." Robins put his gun away. "You wouldn't have any water, would you. I got thrown the second day out, and my canteen is on my horse. The stream here has almost dried up."

"Yes, I carry a few bottles on my sky cycle." Blaze walked over and got one from the utility compartment and took it to Robins.

He opened it and drank deeply.

"You probably got a concussion when you hit that branch. I can get you back home on my cycle, but no room for your horse. I found her a couple miles back."

"I can barely walk; I don't think I could stay on my horse."

"No, that's not a good idea. I'll take you back to town. Someone can come back for your horse."

"Thanks, Ranger. I think I was sent on a wild goose chase. Somebody told me those girls headed west out of town, one of those new guys in town,"

"They were the ones trying to sell them to brothels in the east. They're safe now. I caught two of the *gangers* who were trying to kidnap the girls. Three are still out there somewhere. With any luck, they will keep running back East."

"Millie is probably worried sick, especially since our last sheriff was murdered."

"She was upset when she asked me to look for you." Blaze paused and scanned him with his onboard scanner. It wasn't a medical scanner, but it was sensitive enough to show that Robins didn't have a skull fracture.

"Dixie knows her way home. She was probably heading back to town after she lost me. She's not a bad horse. Something spooked her; it could have been a rattler."

"Can you walk if I help you?"

"Yeah." Robins took his offered hand and let Blaze help him walk to the cycle.

Blaze flew him back to town, and Robin's wife was crying happy tears as she hugged her husband tightly.

Seeing her welcome for Robins made him long to have his own mate in his arms. But if he went home, he would only have a few short hours before he would have to leave again. It was better to stick to the schedule of three days out and two days home.

Before he found Phoebe, he would have just kept traveling from town to town doing his job. He mightn't have seen his home for weeks or months at a time. Finding his mate so early in his new career changed his whole outlook, and his relationship with her was still young.

A single ranger, even one of Blaze's caliber, for this much territory was over-ambitious. He didn't like that he was out doing his job while another cyborg protected his mate.

Fortunately, the next town already had a well-organized police department. They didn't want or need cyborg protectors stationed in their community. However, they were a little concerned about the implications of the Enclave annexing their territory.

Blaze gave them the simple explanation that the Enclave was simply reuniting the parts of the three former countries that had fallen under criminal control subject to human trafficking. He advised them that representatives of the Enclave would be coming to advise how they could benefit the annexed territories' communities. Those representatives would provide them tech that would restore communications within the annex.

TWENTY-TWO

Phoebe found enough to keep herself busy while Blaze was away on the job. Before Stone attempted to lure her back into his clutches, she relished her solitude. As time passed and she got into the routine of caring for her vegetable garden and her livestock, she didn't feel Javen needed to be there while Blaze was working.

Stone was dead. The people who knew Phoebe left with the cyborg ranger would have no way to find her. Blaze vid-called her at least once a day while he was out among the towns. When she tried to discuss letting Javen Black get back to his regular duties, Blaze adamantly refused to consider her arguments.

"But why?" she asked on the latest vid-call. "I took care of myself long before you came along, and before Stone. It was my mistake to get involved with him. But he's dead, and no one associated with him even knows where we live."

"That doesn't mean no one will stumble onto our homestead. There are *gangers* from the East cruising the territory looking for beautiful young females like you," Blaze

185

informed her patiently. "They try luring the females with the promise of a mate to make a family and settle down. Then they kidnap them and transport them East to overlord territory."

"That wouldn't work for me because I am already settled down with you, my love." She gave him a cheeky smile.

Blaze couldn't help smiling at her. In only a couple months, he had fallen completely in love with her. The avatar in his stasis dreams was an apparition compared to his live mate.

"I know you wouldn't go willingly, my mate. These thugs would have no qualms about taking you by force," he said. "They don't come on horses, either. They have hovercrafts and flyers and can have you in overlord territory before I even knew you were gone. Javen stays."

Phoebe sighed in surrender. "Okay. But he's not very good company. I haven't seen another female since I have been with you."

"I put Javen there to protect you, not to be good company," he growled with a fierce look.

She chuckled. "I meant he is no good at making conversation. He will help with any chore I ask, but he hardly ever speaks unless I ask him a direct question."

"That's partly because you are *my* mate and partly because he is there to protect you. He's staying on task."

"The trails are finished, and that bot he brought did a wonderful job taking out the heavy grasses and packing down the dirt. It will be great for riding," Phoebe told him.

"I'm looking forward to walking them with you... But I have found a horse. The farmer who has him hasn't told me what he wants for it. I offered credits. He wasn't interested; they are just numbers to him."

"That's because we've been almost four generations without any kind of monetary units. You have to find out what he needs badly enough to give up one of his horses."

"What about a tractor droid that runs on a crystal drive?"

"I suspect he would not feel comfortable operating it.

"It would work on voice commands."

"I still don't think he would take it. What about a wind turbine or solar collectors? Power to pump water and light his house might be worth more to him."

"That's an excellent idea and cheaper than a tractor droid," Blaze smiled at her. "The new Protectors from the towns I've cleared so far are bringing a load of comm-tablets. I will see that he gets one."

"Can you get one for Sara, too?" Phoebe asked. "At least, I could talk to her until we can visit in person."

"Grafton will be getting Protectors this week who will have comm-tablets to distribute. I will make sure they deliver one to Sara."

"Thank you, Blaze."

"You can thank me in person tomorrow night," he said with a sexy smirk.

"And how might I do that?" she flirted.

"I would rather show you than tell you about it," he said in a low timber that dripped with sexual innuendo.

"Then, I should probably rest up," she said, ending with the kind of pleasurable moan she made when he was doing sexy things to her.

It made him hard to think about it. "Yes, you should get your rest because you can expect to be screaming my name in the wee hours."

"Ooh, I can't wait!" She ended that statement with an air kiss.

It wouldn't be easy for him to wait either.

Phoebe rose early in the mornings when Blaze was out patrolling. He wasn't there keeping her up late at night or in bed until later in the mornings. She missed that when he was away so she kept herself busy with the daily chores of running a homestead. She fed the animals around dawn and went to work in the garden. First, she would pick the produce that was ripe, then she would pull weeds between the plants and the rows.

Javen was always standing watch when she came outside. Cyborgs didn't require nearly as much sleep as natural humans. He would usually sleep for a few hours in whatever vehicle he flew. That would depend on what they might have asked him to pick up on his way to their home.

Well educated in homesteading, he took the initiative with Phoebe's blessing to help with the weeding in the garden. They had just finished the chores before midday when Javen stopped and stood looking up at the sky. Phoebe was closing the gate on the garden fence that was necessary to keep the rabbits from pillaging the garden.

After a moment, she heard the subtle whine of a flyer, but she wasn't alarmed as drones flew over regularly since the Enclave annexed western North America. Still, glancing at Javen a few yards away, she stopped to watch for it. He was frowning, but he didn't say anything. As it came into view on the horizon with the sun behind it, Phoebe couldn't tell what kind of flyer it was.

Without warning, their cabin exploded into a ball of fire. The blast knocked both Phoebe and Javen to the ground, and left her unconscious. Javen rolled to his feet and ran to get Phoebe to safety. Before he could get to her, a high caliber projectile bored a major hole in his chest just below his left pectoral, exiting through his back and slamming him to the ground.

He tried to get up, but he was losing blood so fast he couldn't hold onto consciousness. A normal human would have been killed instantly, but Javen's nanocybots mobilized and stopped the bleeding before he could bleed out. His last conscious thought was to alert Blaze about the attack.

Blaze had just finished meeting with the mayor and village council in the town of Random. They lingered after he relayed the changes in status of the old American western states to chat. A couple of the council members had more questions that they didn't want to air formally during the meeting. One of them was a bit indignant that the Enclave could just come in and tell them what to do.

"As I explained, the Enclave will not be running the town, because I will verify that you are running things in accordance with their criteria..." Blaze stopped mid-sentence and his eyes widened and his sedate expression became one of disbelief and fear. "I have to go!"

With that, he turned and ran out of the village hall and down the street to where he'd parked his sky cycle. He leaped onto it and pinged the starting relate from his CPU. It rose straight into the air while assembling the cockpit. When it was high above the tallest treetops, he gunned it and it took off like a rocket.

Javen had sent him the recording of the explosion and his attempt to get to Phoebe and then nothing.

191

Blaze made the normally forty-minute *flit* in twenty-five minutes. Javen was laying in the grass outside of the garden and his cabin was a pile of smoldering rubble.

He scanned the rubble, fearing what he would find, but she wasn't in there. "Phoebe…" he yelled as he scanned the yard and buildings. He pinged her tablet. It came back from over 200 miles east and moving away fast. Whoever shot Javen and razed his house took her. "Phoeeeebeee!" he screamed. "Phoebe…"

Blaze pushed back the emotions that clouded his thinking and turned his attention to Javen, running to where he lay. Good, he was wearing his weapons belt. Blaze knelt beside him and turned him over.

The needle free syringe was in the pocket where he knew he could find it. It was a bolus of nanites in high protein gel to speed his recovery. His onboard nanites were keeping him alive. They would eventually heal him without intervention, but it might take a week or more by the looks of his horrible wound.

The shooter must have used a large caliber armor piercer round. A few centimeters to the right and it would have pierced his heart and spinal cord. They'd have to tank him in a nanite laced protein bath for that.

Blaze pushed the tip of the syringe into the wound, and pressed the button that released the nanites and protein gel into the hole.

"Commander Dark?" Blaze pinged through the cyborg network and waited.

Minutes passed and Blaze paced beside Javen, waiting for the other cyborg to wake and also a response from their commander.

TWENTY-THREE

"Dark here."

"My homestead has been attacked and they took Phoebe... East 200 miles and counting. That's overlord territory. They shot Javen and blew up our house. How did they even know to come here? This location is classified." Blaze told him.

"It could have been random." Commander Dark suggested.

"No, sir! I think they came for me, and shot Javen, believing he was me,"

"They took her as collateral damage."

"Either way, I'm going after her."

"We have a treaty with the Overlords."

"And I haven't broken it. They did. They took my wife, and they are still moving east. There is nothing in that treaty that says they can destroy my home and take my female without consequences."

"Damn right! But I can't officially support any action to invade Overlord territory."

"I'm calling my team. Meanwhile, you have a spy somewhere in the Enclave. Maybe even a cyborg."

"I will look into it. Ganger incursions don't usually bomb houses and take on cyborgs. It could be anyone. Certain Enclave Personnel have high level access to our AI."

"You do that. I'm calling the team and we are going east."

"It's probably a trap. They've got cyborg naturals who are every bit as deadly as we are."

"I'm sure it is. That's why they took her. They know I will come for her."

"Good luck. Dark out."

"Savage out."

As soon as he broke the connection with Commander Dark, Blaze contacted his team. Fortunately, he had his cache of weapons stored in an underground chamber behind the goat shed. He kept them away from the house because some of his explosives were too volatile to keep in their dwelling.

He wasn't sure what his mission would require, so he took everything his sky cycle could carry, including a small missile launcher with four deceivingly powerful rockets.

While he was doing that, he contacted the other members of his team over the cyborg network. As he gave them the information he got from Javen, a terrible suspicion began to take shape in the back of his mind. What if this was payback for killing Stone?

Of all the people who knew about it, he could only think of two people who might have revealed it to someone outside the Enclave.

Momentarily, Blaze's comm-tablet bleeped in his pocket and he pulled it out immediately. He recognized Sara White as her face appeared on his screen, and she appeared to be crying. "I'm so sorry. I didn't have a choice. They were going to hurt Janie, so I had to tell them."

"That I killed Stone?" Blaze said gruffly. "But you didn't tell them where to find us. You couldn't have because you didn't know. It's not your fault Sara. The location of our home was only known to a few people associated with the Enclave. Someone there leaked the information, so don't blame yourself."

"What are you going to do?" Sarah asked.

"I'm going to get her back or die trying."

#

Phoebe awoke to the soft whine of a flyer engine. She was tied to a passenger seat behind the pilot.

"Who are you? Where are you taking me? Why did you blow up my house?"

"Knowing who I am will have no meaning to you. I am following orders, and I am taking you to the man who gave those orders. He will tell you what he wants you to know."

"Who is this man? What does he want with me?" Phoebe blurted.

"Edmund Stone. I don't know why he wants you."

"Oh, no!" she exclaimed softly. "Omigod!" She closed her eyes and leaned her head back against the seat. "He's going to kill me."

If the pilot heard what she said, he gave no indication. She could only hope Blaze would find out in time to stop Edmund Stone. Then she realized that was exactly what Stone wanted. He had her kidnapped to set a trap for Blaze.

197

Blaze was the target. He was going to use her to hurt Blaze for killing his brother? Son? It didn't matter, now she knew what this was all about.

And she had told Blaze she didn't need Javen to protect her, that she could take care of herself. She was tied so tight; she couldn't even reach into her pocket to get her comm-tablet. Then she realized they let her keep it so Blaze could trace her location and come after her.

Her eyes filled with angry tears at her helplessness to stop what seemed about to happen. Blaze would come after her, she just had to stay alive until he did.

Phoebe had no idea how long or how far they had traveled when the flyer landed because she had been unconscious for part of the trip. The last thing she remembered was seeing a small rocket hit their cabin. What happened to Javen? Were the animals injured? Who would help them if they were?

She didn't get to see the pilot's face until they landed. He was big and powerful like Blaze, but he looked older. His facial expression was neutral as he unfastened her from the seat and zip tied her hands behind her as soon as she was on her feet.

As he helped her from the flyer, she saw they had landed by what could only be described as a mansion on a couple of acres surrounded by a high chain link fence and thick woods on all sides. The unnamed man gripped her upper arm and led her in through the back door of the building.

Once inside they didn't stop, but continued through the kitchen to a wide stairway and started up the stairs, pulling her with him. Even with him holding her arm, climbing the stairs was difficult and she stumbled a couple times. The man guiding her said nothing, pausing for her to regain her balance and continue up the stairs.

At the top of the stairs stood a man who bore a striking resemblance to Martin Stone. Phoebe sucked in her breath, willing herself to breathe slowly even though she felt on the verge of panic.

"Martin said you were beautiful. This is going to be more entertaining than I imagined. Too bad he's not here to enjoy and share this pleasure."

Omigod! He's going to rape me.

"He was a sick son of a bitch whose greatest pleasure was hurting me."

He slapped her face so fast she never saw it coming. She grunted in pain, but refused to give him any further satisfaction. "Put her in the restraint frame." Stone said.

The man holding her arm pulled her along with him as he entered the open doorway a few feet ahead of them. As she saw what the room contained, she tried to resist the man trying to steer her inside. She saw some of the same torture machines and restraining devices as Martin had used on her.

"No, please don't do this. I didn't do anything. Let me go! Let me go!"

The big man said the first words since he'd taken her. "I'm sorry. I have my orders."

He wrapped his arms around her and carried her into the room and set her down by a heavy rectangular pipe frame with four leather cuffs attached overhead. Despite her struggles against his restraint, she failed to stop him from cuffing her wrists and ankles to the frame, spread eagle.

The man frowned when he finished, turned without a word and strode from the room.

At least he left her still wearing the khaki green t-shirt and black cargo pants, the only clothing in her wardrobe. It was hard to gauge the amount of time she spent in the room alone trussed up in that frame. Long enough for her arms and legs and back to ached with fatigue. She also had a few bruises from being thrown to the ground by the blast.

She was tired, thirsty, and scared. Whatever happened, she had to hold herself together and stay alive long enough for Blaze to get there.

Just when Phoebe managed to calm herself and strengthen her resolve, Edmund came into the room carrying a short black wand and a small knife, a very sharp looking knife. He smiled and stroked her cheek with the back of the blade.

He was just taunting her. Phoebe stood completely still and followed the knife with her eyes. Edmond laughed, pulling out the neckline of her t-shirt as far as it would stretch, then he cut through the fabric from the neckline through the hem. Pushing the sides apart, he stared at her breasts supported by a simple fabric bra.

Stone lifted the stretchy fabric away from her flesh and cut through it with his knife. He pushed the sides apart, and Phoebe turned her head and closed her eyes as he stopped to admire his work.

"Open your eyes, slut." He grabbed her chin and forced her face forward. "Look at me."

Phoebe obeyed, glaring at him defiantly, forcing herself not to react when he gripped her breasts and squeezed them hard. He just laughed and released them. Stone finished cutting off her shirt and bra, then went to work on her pants and panties.

When she was naked, except for her boots, he stepped back to admire his work. "Oh yeah. I'm going to have a lot of fun with you."

Phoebe cringed inwardly. That's what Martin said before he inflicted pain that he called discipline. "But first we call your mate and show him what we've done with you."

Stone had put away the knife and he held up her tablet in one hand and the black wand in the other hand. "Give the command to call your mate."

"Call Blaze," she obeyed, hoping at least to see his face, afraid to hope he would get her out of there. She knew he would try.

"Phoebe, where are you?" Blaze answered immediately.

"Blaze," Phoebe said.

"Yes, Captain Savage. Your lovely mate is my guest. I know that you killed my brother. Martin had his faults, but he was family. If you value your female… If you want her to live you will be here by midnight.

Stone made sure he saw Phoebe naked and restrained, then he touched the wand to her upper abdomen. As he held it there, searing pain surged through her body. It hurt so bad she could only scream in agony, until she passed out.

"I'm on my way," Blaze ground out. *You are going to die!*

TWENTY-FOUR

Phoebe opened her eyes and scanned her surroundings. It hadn't been a dream; it was a nightmare come true. She was still in Edmund Stone's torture chamber. Every muscle in her body ached, and her throat was raw from screaming. She even suspected she had lost control of her bladder when he used that pain stick on her. She didn't have to pee any more.

She was stretched so tight in this torture frame of his that she could barely move. The pain device had caused all her major muscles to cramp at once, setting her nerves on fire.

Blaze was coming. She just had to hold on a little longer and it would be over. She closed her eyes and thought about how safe and loved she felt in his arms. How much she had come to love him. He would be here soon. She just had to hold on a little longer.

Footsteps… Someone was coming. Phoebe's eyes opened wide. Stone was back.

He was carrying a glass of clear liquid with a straw in it. She hoped it was water, though she feared it was poison. He put the straw to his own lips and sipped, swallowing the liquid before he put it to her lips. She drank greedily before he took it away. It had been hours since she had anything to eat or drink. But she needed water more than food. She would have drained the glass it he hadn't taken it away. He only let her have about fifty cc.

"We wouldn't want you to embarrass yourself again," Stone said with a contemptuous smile. He set the glass aside and took out the horrible black wand again. He gave one end a little twist and started stroking her body with it length wise.

Phoebe flinched every time he touched her with it. He ran it *all* over her body, between her legs over her breasts. He wasn't hurting her; he was taunting her, lulling her before he went back to torture. The second she relaxed, he applied the business end, all the places he'd stroked her with it, inflicting painful little shocks, eliciting little cries in response. The last was so excruciating she let out a scream ending in sobs.

Gunfire. Phoebe choked back her sobs to listen. Gunfire repeated again and again. Blaze was out there! Stone stopped tormenting her and put his hand to his ear, listening. His disdainful grin confirmed it.

"I'm sorry we won't have much more time to play, but your mate is here just in time to watch you die."

"And then you die," she asserted hoarsely. Then she shrieked as he hit her with another jolt, and laughed.

As the gunfire continued with intermittent reports from ion rifles, Stone went back to tormenting her with little shocks from the pain wand. When the gunfire stopped, Stone stopped to listen again, nodding.

"Send him up, alone and unarmed." He twisted the end of the wand again then jabbed the end into Phoebe just above her belly button and she screamed loud and long.

#

Edmond Stone's first mistake was taking Phoebe. His second was calling to taunt him and torturing her with pain sticks on holovid. The call gave Blaze the location of Stone's compound. He knew it was a trap, but he was going anyway with his ranger team backing him.

They landed their sky cycles about half a mile away and walked through the heavily wooded area surrounding Stone's mansion compound. They used their knives to take out the armed guards patrolling the perimeter outside the high voltage chain link fence.

Stalker used a laser tool to cut through the fence, then they used insulated gloves to pull the side open. As soon as they cut the fence, an alarm sounded for the security breech.

Blaze's team lunged through the opening one at a time and ran to their positions surrounding the mansion, carrying their ion rifles. The guards outside the mansion fired on the armor-clad cyborg. Their bullets stung on impact, but didn't penetrate their armor.

Once the cyborg rangers were in position, they fired back on the Stone's guards and downed them all.

With the other five cyborgs in position, Blaze was going in through the front door. Darken Hawk had his back. While their armor would resist penetration by ion rifles, prolonged blasts would cause damage.

Blaze pulled open the front door, breaking off some of the door frame with it. Armed gangers fired armor piercing bullets that bounced off his armor. He fired his rifle, sweeping the area with repeating blasts and the hail of gunfire stopped.

Echoes of gunfire from both kinds of weapons reverberated through the house while the alarm continued to blast repeatedly. Blaze and Darken took out every being who challenged them. By then the other four Cyborg rangers reported they had entered the building and were going room to room clearing the opposition.

Falcon Rader hacked into the security system and killed the alarm. So far, they had cleared all the rooms on the first floor, without finding Phoebe.

Blaze paused and scanned for the nanites he had transferred to her during their kissing and breeding. *"Upstairs."*

"Stairway that way." Max Steel pointed to the left.

"Darken, take point. I'm going in through the back.

Led by Darken, the rest of the team headed to the stairs, ion rifles poised and ready to shoot. Three armed and armored cyborgs blocked the way. Blaze's cohorts all pointed their rifles at them.

"Blaze Savage?" The one in the middle questioned.

"Yeah, what?" Darken answered.

"Mr. Stone said you should go upstairs alone, unarmed if you want to see your female alive again."

"Why? So, he can kill her in front of me?"

The other cyborg didn't answer. A blood curdling feminine scream and crying came from upstairs.

"Or you can stay down here and listen to her scream while he uses the pain stick on her."

Darken gave his rifle to Shadow and took off his weapon belt and pulled four throwing knives from secret sheaths in his armor. He dropped them all onto the floor, but only retracted his helmet to reveal his midnight blue eyes. When the three rogues were satisfied, he was unarmed, they let Darken pass.

As Darken climbed the stairs, another blood curdling scream echoed through the house.

Blaze launched the grappling hook up to the second-floor window sill just as he heard Phoebe scream again. He clenched his jaw and climbed up the rope as fast and silently as he could. When he reached the window to see inside, he had to tamp down his emotions.

His mate was trussed up naked in what could only be called a bondage frame. Stone had the pain stick in his hand and was about to press the business end against her spine. Blaze, pulled out his blaster, punched through the window glass and shot Stone.

Stone's head exploded into gore that hit both Phoebe and the rogue cyborg as Darken stepped into the room.

Blaze levered himself, and lunged through the remainder of the window. The rogue, splattered in the side of his face with Stone's brain matter, turned in time to his see boss man's body slump to the floor with his whole head split open.

He turned with the blaster he'd pointed at Darken and pointed it at Blaze.

"Do you really want to do that?" Blaze pointed his blaster at his unprotected face.

He glanced at the remains of Stone on the floor, and lowered his weapon. "No point. Take your female and get out of here. This was his grudge, not mine. He had it coming. He would have killed her just like the others. We can run this place fine without him, and the women will live to entertain other clients."

Blaze tossed Darken his blaster and took out his knife. Squatting in front of Phoebe, he cut the straps holding her ankles. "Phee, I got you," he murmured and cut the straps holding her arms.

TWENTY-FIVE

"Blaze help!" she moaned. "Make him stop."

"It's over Baby. I'm going to get you out of here," he said softly by her ear. He sheathed his knife, glancing around the room looking for her clothes.

The whole room was lined with various BDSM equipment much like Martin Stone's dungeon. He spotted the remnants of her clothes in a pile on the floor. He reached for a small tube in a loop on his weapon's belt. Popping the top off with his thumb, a silvery piece of fabric poked up. It expanded in to a thin sheet as he pulled it out.

Wrapping it around Phoebe he picked her up in his arms and carried her from the room with Darken watching his back as he had descended the stairs. The rogue cyborgs and his team were no longer at a standoff. The rogues stepped aside as Blaze carried his mate downstairs.

Blaze nodded to them as he passed. He didn't think about why they were letting them go without a fight until much later. As he strode out into the night, Phoebe put her arms around him, hid her face against his shoulder, and wept softly. After everything Stone had done to her, he knew she needed to let it out.

It tore at him that he'd had a part in her suffering, because he killed Martin Stone. His brother took revenge by hurting Phoebe. So, his gratitude that the rogues let them go without a fight was limited. They had kidnapped her for their boss to torture.

If he and his team fought and killed the rogues when it was unnecessary, someone else might come for revenge. They had already left enough bodies behind. That made too many variables to accurately calculate the odds of retribution for the dead gangers.

Blaze didn't care about his home. There was nothing contained inside that could not be replaced. He'd arranged for temporary shelter on his way to rescue Phoebe. He knew she would need a place to rest and recover when they got back. Her damage was more mental than physical, from his scan of her.

He carried Phoebe through the woods all the way back to where they'd left their sky cycles.

"Do you think she will be all right?" Darken asked as they walked.

"With time, I think so," Blaze said grimly. "That deviant was as evil as his brother."

"The rogue cyborgs downstairs told us it was an exclusive club for BDSM, but Stone had killed some of their best females by taking things too far," said Falcon.

"They seemed not to mind that you killed him," said Shadow.

"They blew up my home, kidnapped my mate for Stone then they let us go after I killed Stone, like we did them a favor. What am I missing?" Blaze asked.

"Cyborg rangers came back for them when their units were forced to leave them behind. Rangers held off the Mesaarkans so med evac could pick them up." Falcon said. "They didn't know you were a cyborg ranger when Stone gave them the orders."

"Even after we killed their gangers?"

"They were Stone's gangers," Falcon said. "That's how they saw it."

"Thank you all for your help," Blaze said.

"You would do the same for us," Darken said and the others confirmed his statement.

"Yes, I would," Blaze said as they reached their vehicles. "I'm taking her to Medic Knox Brakar in Birch Hollow. He is the closest."

"Let us know if you need *anything*," said Darken. He and the others went to their cycles while Blaze set Phoebe astride his.

Blaze held her upper arm to keep her from falling over while he reached into the cargo compartment to pull out one of his spare t-shirts to cover her better than just the thin sheet. After he put it on her, he climbed on behind her and pulled her against his chest. Using his interface with the computer to extend the wings and close the cockpit, he wrapped his arms around Phoebe and hugged her.

"I've got you now, Phee. You're going to get through this. I'm going to help you in every way I can," he murmured into her ear.

"Blaze, I knew you would come." She put her arms over his and relaxed against him. He nuzzled her neck and kissed her there.

He continued to hold her as his sky cycle lifted into the air and flew off into the night. It took less than an hour to get to Birch Hollow at high speed.

Despite the late hour, Medic Knox Brakar's storefront office was fully lit as open for business as they landed. By the time Blaze retracted the cockpit and carried Phoebe to the door, Knox was holding open it for him to enter.

"Let's take her right in for a full scan and we can go from there," said Knox, leading the way to a room in the back. "Can you stand her on that white circle?"

"I'm okay," Phoebe murmured.

"Don't move, until I say," said Knox.

She managed to hold herself steady for the fifteen seconds it took to complete it. When she started to sway on her feet, Blaze caught her in his arms so she wouldn't fall.

"Let's go into the treatment room. Other than some bruises, dehydration, and fatigue. There are no serious physical problems." Knox stated. "But it's evident she's suffered emotional shock."

Blaze picked up his mate and carried her into the treatment room and laid her on the padded table.

"He tortured her with a pain stick," Blaze ground out. "She passed out for a time, but she doesn't know for how long…"

"No evidence of rape," Knox answered before Blaze could finish. "Phoebe, will you let me give you some fluids and some medication to lessen the emotional trauma you've suffered. It won't erase the memory, just make it seem like something that happened a long time ago."

"Yes please," she said with a sigh.

"We have a two-bed infirmary here. After I give you the medications, I'd like to give you a sedative and have you rest until tomorrow. My mate will pick up a set of standard issue clothing, before we open the office in the morning."

"That sounds like a good idea," said Blaze.

"I apologize that there is only a bed for one," said Knox.

"No problem," said Blaze. "We would go a week or more without sleep during the war. I will stay with her."

Blaze went to Phoebe's side and took her hand, bending down to kiss her forehead. "Phee, I am so sorry he hurt you. Javen alerted me as he was shot down, and I left immediately."

"How did they find us?" Phoebe asked. "Our location was confidential."

"It had to be someone in the Enclave, connected to the Overlord syndicate. Our communications run through separate channels. Only the shuttle port in New Chicago has a direct channel to the Starport in Farringay, and the Overlords run their communications through the Starport. There are a limited number of people who have access to both. Obviously, someone leaked it to Stone." Blaze explained. "Martin's man Clade probably found his comm-tablet and told Edmond; I killed his brother."

"Clade doesn't do anything for nothing. He got a reward for telling Edmond who killed his brother," Phoebe replied.

"Odds are, we will find Clade no longer lives in Grafton. He knows I would suspect him first for telling Stone I killed his brother," Blaze said in a somber tone. "Phee, I never would have killed him, if I believed it would come back on you."

"It was that or prison offworld. Edmond wouldn't have made that distinction. He meant to kill me in front of you, she mused. "Who was the guy in front of me while you came in from the back? He looks so much like you; it took me a second to realize it wasn't."

"Darken Hawk. He's my genetic brother, but we aren't twins. He volunteered, because we calculated that Stone was more likely to kill you first. That gave me enough time to get into position."

Knox returned with a bag of intravenous medicine. "I've included a bolus of nanites to help heal the bruising. There is an infuser in the patient room so Phoebe can get comfortable while I hook it up."

Blaze picked her up again to carry her to the next room.

"Blaze, I can still walk," she protested.

"I know, but I want to carry you."

"Okay," she said with a sigh and put her arms around his neck, indulging him.

Once she was settled in bed, it took Knox just a minute to insert the IV. When the infusion finished, the nanites would disengage the tiny tube and close the vein. Within a few minutes of starting the medication, Phoebe became sleepy and drifted to sleep as Blaze held her hand.

TWENTY-SIX

Phoebe woke when it was almost mid-day to find Blaze still sitting beside her. A new set of clothing was waiting on the end of the bed as promised.

She was a little disoriented due to the medication she was given to prevent post-traumatic stress. It left her feeling like she had lost a chunk of time overnight. The fact that she awoke in a strange place added to her confusion, but she was relieved and happy to find Blaze at her side when she hadn't expected him for a couple days.

Sitting up, she started to get out of bed and realized she was wearing only one of Blaze's t-shirts. "Where are we? What happened to my clothes?"

"You were kidnapped and they were destroyed."

"But that was a while ago."

"The medic gave you meds to make if feel like that to make it easier to deal with it. Do you remember who took you?"

"Edmond Stone's man. They blew up our house. Stone cut off my clothes," she said and shivered. "And he used a pain stick. He was a fucking pervert just like his brother. You killed him."

"Yes," Blaze admitted. "That was yesterday." He said the last reluctantly.

"Okay, but it doesn't feel like yesterday. I feel like it was last year, even though I didn't know you then." She got up from the bed and stepped in front of him as he sat in the chair beside the bed. Draping her arms around his neck, she gave him a light kiss on his lips. "I missed you so much. Can we go home, now? I really need you to fuck me."

Blaze groaned and pulled her onto his lap and claimed her lips in a torrid kiss. "Ah, Phee, I need that, too." He hugged her fervently, then set her away, and helped her to her feet. "Knox's mate brought you some clothes. Get dressed and I will take you to our temporary home."

"Oh, yeah. They blew it up." She walked over to the end of the bed and looked through the neat pile and found the panties which she pulled on first. "Is Javen all right?"

"He will be. The cyborg who blew up our house and took you shot him. That disabled him long enough for him to get to you."

"That's awful! I'm glad Medic Knox shifted my memories. The animals. Did any of them get hurt?"

"They're fine. Javen checked on them when he was healed enough to get up and around," Blaze told her as she pulled on the standard issue black cargo pants.

She turned away from him and pulled off his t-shirt then put on the stretch bra and her new t-shirt.

Blaze frowned when she turned back to face him.

"I didn't want to tease you since we need to leave." She shrugged and smiled at him.

They found Medic Knox and his wife at the reception desk out front.

"You look well rested. I'm Nancy. Knox is my husband."

"Thank you both. I feel good, and thanks for the clothes."

"Don't mention it. We charged them to Blaze's account."

The two women shared a conspiratorial chuckle.

"It's too bad you're all the way out in old Texas. There's a group of cyborg wives here and we get together every few weeks to socialize."

"That sounds like fun. I don't even know where Birch Hollow is from our homestead."

"About three hours at top speed with the sky cycle. But you can always call Nancy. Stalker recovered your comm-tablet. It's in the cargo compartment."

Yes, do call," Nancy encouraged. "If you can't come in person, you can join us by com. Some of the other cyborg wives have settled in remote locations. If you need anything, or just need to talk, comm me."

"Thank you, I will."

"Thanks for everything, both of you," Blaze said. "We are going home to prepare for my new horse and a new house."

The flight back to their homestead was uneventful. This time Phoebe rode cuddled against Blaze's back with her arms wrapped around his waist. He shuddered at the memory of how close he'd been to losing her.

How many more local tyrants had connections with the Eastern Overlords and the tech to contact them directly? Now that he knew the location of his homestead was leaked, he would take further steps to secure the property.

When they arrived at the homestead, Javen had finished setting up their temporary housing, complete with bathroom facilities and running water. The shelter was even smaller than their tiny one room cabin. It was more like a cabin on a starship, a bedroom with a small sitting area and a fold out table for eating. There was no food processor, only a small refrigeration unit for drinks and a supply of meal bars.

As they landed beside the shelter and Blaze retracted the cockpit, Phoebe's dog Brandy came trotting out to greet them, barking softly. Her horse came over to the fence across from the new shelter and nickered.

Phoebe climbed off the cycle and squatted to hug her dog and pet her. "I am so glad you were not hurt." Brandy licked her face in return.

She stood and looked over the goat pasture and the chickens roaming the yard. Then her gaze fell on the rubble of their cabin. The sight left her feeling like it had been stolen from them. It had become home in the few months she had lived there with Blaze. Angry tears pricked her eyes.

"I don't blame you, baby. I'd like to go back and punch whichever of Stone's cyborgs blew up our house and kidnapped you."

"It doesn't matter. You killed the man responsible." Phoebe moved to his side and put her arms around his waist and leaned against him."

"Javen has arranged for machines to come tomorrow to clear the rubble away. We will look at construction kits for our new home on my comm-tablet."

"When do you have to go back out on recon?" Phoebe asked, looking up at him.

"Not for a few weeks. I must be sure you will be safe here while I am away. I contacted Commander Dark and asked for a trained protector team to start clearing towns for Enclave personnel."

"I'm so glad. I miss you so much when you are gone," she said, hugging him.

"It's hard for me to leave you every time. Let's go inside, and I will show you just how much I missed you."

"Yeah," she said and let him steer her into the new shelter.

Inside, a large bed dominating the space drew her attention, then she noted the open door to the bathroom to the left. She went inside to use it, and it was tiny. Even though it had a shower, it seemed way too small for them to make love in.

When she returned to the bedside, Blaze had removed his shirt. For a moment, Phoebe was mesmerized by the mouth-watering view of his chest and washboard abs.

Her nipples grew taut, prickling for contact his hard chest pressing against them. She smiled up at him and pulled her own shirt untucked and off over her head, followed by her bra.

"You are so beautiful," he said softly. "Are you sure?"

"That I want you? Oh, yes. I'm sure, sweetheart. What happened yesterday doesn't quite seem real. This is real, Blaze. I love you and I want you to fuck me until I barely know my own name." she told him and laughed.

"I can do that." He stepped close to her and took her face between his hands and kissed her until they were both breathless with arousal. Then they hurried to finish stripping off their clothing.

Phoebe got on the bed first and moved to the middle without turning it down. She spread her legs so Blaze could lay over her between them.

It still seemed surreal to know what happened to her the day before, but without feeling the emotional trauma. The days he'd been away that she longed to have him in her arms like this were at the forefront of her thoughts.

After another passionate kiss, Phoebe said, "now, Blaze. I need you inside me now."

"As you wish, my love," he murmured and slid his cock into her wet, welcoming pussy.

They moaned in utter relief at finally being joined again. Phoebe wanted Blaze in Alpha mode, surrendering to him completely. Lacing his fingers through hers, he held her hands against the bed while he loomed over her.

Phoebe mewled, arching her back to rub her aching nipples against his chest. As he pressed his chest to hers, relishing that contact, he claimed her mouth in a fierce, dominating kiss. Her response was just as spirited as she squeezed his cock with her inner walls.

Her whole body throbbed for him to press down on her and pound into her. She stared up into his eyes when he freed her kiss swollen lips and his look enraptured her with his sexual prowess. His eyes were dark with passion and raw need. They told her without words that he would give her all that she desired on his own terms, to which she was more than willing to surrender.

She had him right where she wanted him.

TWENTY-SEVEN

He drew his cock almost out and rammed it back into her hitting both her sweet spot and her clit.

She huffed and aahed as he lowered his hard chest against her breasts. He repeated the movement intermittently between long demanding kisses. Soon he held her on the precipice of orgasm, where he teased her with the promise of release.

Phoebe panted and moaned with extreme arousal, wondering what he wanted in exchange for release.

"Blaze... Please... I need..."

"Don't worry, baby. I'm going to give it to you." He kissed her tenderly, releasing her hands and running his thumbs over her taut, erect nipples. He thrust in and out of her several times. She put her arms around him, caressing his head and neck. As he felt her muscles tightening against him, he ended the kiss and watched her face as he pinched her nipples.

Phoebe met his gaze and gasped. "Yes, Blaze!" it wasn't quite a scream. But he looked pleased with himself as she came, squeezing him hard as her body was racked by powerful contractions of her womb. "Oh, Blaze, my precious love. I missed you." She hugged him with her arms and legs and inner walls, whispering, "I love you. I am yours, and I love you."

Blaze already knew that but it felt so good to hear her say the words out loud, so he said it back to her. "I am yours, and I love you, too."

She smiled up at him, and he kissed her, slipping his tongue into her mouth to caress and tease hers in a tender duel. By the time his mouth parted from hers, the aftershocks of her climax had finished.

Blaze caressed her cheeks with his fingers and planted a soft kiss on her lips. "Are you ready?"

She nodded.

He pulled out and rose on his knees as she turned over and crouched on her knees and forearms. She looked back at him and wiggled her ass, offering her pussy for his pleasure. Blaze moved in closer and pushed the head of his cock against her entrance.

Phoebe pushed back against him as he grasped her hips and slid all the way in. She let out a long, "Aah" as it bumped her cervix.

Blaze leaned over her and cupped her breasts in his hands, kneading them and plucking at her erect nipples before he began fucking her again. He started pumping in and out of her at a leisurely rhythm, long driving strokes. Steadily faster, he thrust his cock into her, so hard his balls slapped against her clit.

With Blaze, she loved a good hard fucking. As she had gotten to know him in the last several months, she became confident that he would never take it too far. He didn't have to hurt her to have an orgasm. No cyborg would deliberately harm his mate or find pleasure in it.

He found joy in her pleasure as well as his own. When he took her into rapture, she did scream his name, and she came again as he came inside her, his hot seed pouring into her womb.

He stayed inside her as long as he could, pulsing his cock to stimulate more contractions in her waning orgasm. When he finally withdrew, he leaned over her again and hug her with one hand gripping her breast and his forearm against her other.

"It's so good to be home."

"It's so good to have you."

He smiled and kissed the back of her neck.

As they lay together afterward, Blaze on his back with Phoebe nestled against his side, her head on his shoulder, he flashed back on the events of the day before. He remembered the stark terror when Javen reported what had happened. It had paralyzed him for a minute or two, the utter fear at the possibility he would lose her forever.

Blaze had reverted to the emotion dampeners programmed into his CPU, putting her rescue into the context of a mission, so he could organize it. Once Phoebe was safe in his arms, he wished there had been the chance to make Edmond Stone suffer for his crimes as his brother had.

Worse, he realized he could not have stopped the initial attack any more Javen had. Armor piercing bullets could penetrate their metal alloy rib cage when they hit just right. And what if Phoebe had been inside the house when they blew it up?

Even if they moved to a new location, it could get leaked again. They didn't know yet how Edmond Stone learned their homestead's location. Cyborg weren't mind readers, but they could usually tell when someone was lying to them. They didn't even know who to question.

Blaze knew he would rather die himself than lose Phoebe. That was so he wouldn't know the pain of losing her. That would surely kill him. Somehow, he needed to resolve these feelings, or he could never go back to work or leave Phoebe's side.

There had to be a way to learn who leaked the location. The eastern overlords' communications were on separate satellites from the Enclave's. However, the New Chicago Space Shuttle Port was on both satellites because of their connection with the Starport in Farringay.

The only way an Enclave comm could connect with an Overlord comm would be to run the signal through both spaceports. There would be records in the AI servers. So, he contacted Commander Dark to ask for one of their AI technicians to search for the origins of such communications during the time span between his killing Martin Stone and the attack on the homestead.

Blaze suspected whoever was responsible for leaking the coordinates to his homestead would be found in that analysis. Even then, he wouldn't feel confident that Phoebe would be safe here whether he was home or not.

Maybe he should have taken the same treatment as Phoebe to cope with the trauma of her kidnapping and the destruction of their home. He was obsessing on his fear and he couldn't seem to get it under control. Blaze drew in a deep breath and let it out slowly, repeating it a few times.

There were things he could do to make their homestead safe. A complete security system with cameras and anti-aircraft drones, maybe some security droids to feed information to her cyborg bodyguard. They'd had no warning that the flyer they heard could be dangerous.

With warning, Javen may have been able to take down the flyer with his ion rifle. Or at least disable it. An anti-aircraft drone could have taken it down. It would be expensive, but credits were worth nothing to him without *her*.

Finally, he began to relax and closed his eyes. He'd made a plan.

TWENTY-EIGHT

Phoebe awoke alone in the bed sometime later and stretched, just a little sore from making love with Blaze. She smiled as she heard the shower. Getting up, she padded to the bathroom, barefoot and naked. Once she had relieved herself, she squeezed into the shower behind Blaze and hugged him.

"Good morning," she murmured, pressing a kiss to his spine. "That was some night."

Blaze paused the shower, setting it to a fine warm mist. As soon as she pressed her naked body against him, he went hard. The way she was moving her hands over his chest and abdomen told him; she wanted him again.

He turned and lifted her against the shower wall and leaned into her. She wrapped her arms and legs around him as he took her mouth in a heated kiss, the length of his cock pressed against her wet heat. It didn't seem to bother him that there was barely room to move. Fortunately, the shower head was in the ceiling and rotated on command.

Without breaking the kiss, he maneuvered his cock at her entrance and sank it into her. She moaned into his mouth as he took her hard and fast, cradling her buttocks in his hands to cushion her back against the flexible wall.

Phoebe clung to him, murmuring her pleasure with soft little moans in the rhythm of his thrusts, wailing her satisfaction as he took them to orgasm together.

"Good morning," he said with a sexy smile, pulsing his cock inside her.

She laughed in agreement, caressing his shoulders and neck. "I love waking up with you." She framed his face in her hands and kissed his lips lightly. "I love you," She added with certainty.

Hearing the words and seeing them in the way she looked at him filled Blaze's heart with joy. He had taken this job as a favor to Commander Vyken Dark, but reluctantly. Now he believed it was the best decision he ever made.

Blaze had fallen in love with her that first day, knowing she was his genetic mate. He felt fortunate to have found her, knowing that probably half a million cyborgs were still waiting.

They finished their shower and dressed, sharing a breakfast of juice, wishing for coffee. Their supply was lost with the cabin.

"I finally heard from Sara," said Phoebe, who was sipping her juice intermittently. "She wants to know when I can come down for a visit."

"We could probably fly down for the day, the beginning of the week after next. My new horse is coming Friday. The owner was happy to trade for a small wind turbine and a solar array."

"Did you ask him about the droid tractor?"

"I did, and you were right. He wasn't interested. It didn't come with the attachments that he already had for his horse team."

"What about tack for the horse?"

"It's coming by drone in a few days. I had to have it made special. It cost almost as much as the horse."

"Clydesdales are big. I can't wait to see him."

"He's a nice horse... Seemed to like me and carried me with little trouble."

"Good thing you are tall; I would never be able to saddle him."

"We could set up a block and tackle for that in case you ever needed to." He suggested.

"Wouldn't hurt," she said. "Want to go out and take a look at the new trail Javen made for us?"

"I do."

"Good, because I know what will happen if we stay here."

He gave her a wicked grin. "Who says it can't happen out there?"

Phoebe laughed as she got up to put their dishes into the cleaner. "It wouldn't be the first time."

As soon as she'd finished, they stepped outside into the sun. It was a warm fall day. The horse and the goats were in the pasture with chickens foraging in the yard outside it. Phoebe's dog trotted up to greet them, and she paused to pet Brandy.

The dog followed them down the new trail as they strolled together hand in hand.

"This place is really starting to feel like home," she told him. "Well, before they blew up the house."

"It was. I had a place on Phantom with a small plot of land. It was comfortable, but I didn't feel at home like I do here with you. Most of the men I served with were there, and we would congregate for games and working out."

"Sounds lonely."

"The first couple of years, I needed that solitude to come down out of warrior mode. When I did, I ran a projection of my life on Phantom, and all I could see was endless days stretching ahead filled with the monotony of sameness. Then I got the call from Commander Dark," he said.

"I was just getting myself back from the nightmare with Martin when his men showed up with the note from him. After what Sara told me, I knew it was a lie. I had already seen his dark side. You did the town a favor, getting rid of him."

"I only wish I had arrived before he hurt you," he said, stopping. He turned to her and lifted her in his arms, holding her against his chest, kissing her spontaneously.

Phoebe parted her lips to welcome his gentle caress. He was holding back, as it was a showing of affection rather than a prelude to breeding. Even though they were both holding back their passion for each other, that sweet kiss was still arousing.

She could kiss him for hours and never get tired of him. As much as she enjoyed his tenderness, she didn't object when he pulled back reluctantly and let her slide down his body until her feet were back on the ground.

"My sweet mate," he smiled at her as he framed her face in his hands. "I'm saving a whole lot more for later."

"I'm counting on it," she laughed softly because she could feel his unmistakable erection against her belly as well as her female parts on high alert.

They started walking again, on the path that encompassed the whole property's perimeter, a little over five miles.

"There are a few branches we will need to trim on the path for horseback riding, especially with you riding a Clydesdale. I hope Sherry likes him."

"From all I have learned about horses, his breed seems easygoing."

"Are you going to keep his name 'Arthur?'"

"Why not? It's a strong name. He was named for the legend of King Arthur because they thought a horse of his strength and size was needed for a knight in full armor."

"But, they're not?"

"They aren't. In medieval times, they used smaller horses. Arthur seems to fit him."

"As long as you are happy with it."

They had walked for a while when they came to another path cut perpendicular to the one, they walked. "Where does this path go?"

"I forgot to tell you; we made some shortcuts. This path on the left leads across the center of the property. We made another one that cut through the middle perpendicular to this one. I asked Javen to do that so we would have more route variations."

"I see you have been keeping him busy."

"He was happy to have something to do. It's gotta be boring for him to stand guard on me three days on and two days off," she mused. "Don't you think you are overly cautious?

"Phoebe, they blew up our house and kidnapped you! I don't want something worse to happen," he reminded.

243

"I'm sorry. The treatment pushed it back in my memory… Like that happened before Martin."

"For me, it happened yesterday…"

Blaze had a haunted look that she had never seen before, not even when he talked about war.

Phoebe put her arms around his waist and hugged him, pressing her cheek against his chest. "I'm sorry. I wasn't thinking how it was for you. Believe me, I would feel the same, my mate."

"Javen stays! And we are getting a whole security system. I decided last night. I will never be able to do my job, unless I know you will be safe on our own homestead."

"No, you're right. I just feel bad for Javen. He clearly feels awkward around me."

"Because you are not his female, and he doesn't want to disrespect me by acting inappropriately."

"Well, you sure don't have to worry about that. Javen is very proper. I wish he had a female. At least I would have someone to talk to."

"You can vid-call Sara on your comm-tablet," Blaze reminded.

"She did call me. I don't think about her having one," she said. "I haven't had one that long. I just think in terms of talking to you with it while you're out on the job."

"Since she called you, her code is in your tablet, so you can call her back."

"I planned to do that tomorrow after you go."

"But I'm not going back to work for a few weeks."

"I'll call her later to let her know when we are coming."

Blaze hugged her back and kissed the top of her head. "Although it's a long shot, let's go back and order our new house, then see if we can salvage anything from the old one."

TWENTY-NINE

"Hey, Sara! It's so good to see you. How are Joanie and Janie?" Phoebe smiled at the image of Sara on her comm-tablet.

"They're fine. Things are a little tight without my job, but I don't miss *him*. My girls have grown up so much this year he was starting to look at them differently... I think you know what I mean."

"Ooh, yeah. That's a little creepy."

"That's what they said," she replied.

"I saw the signs. I feel like I should have known things weren't right." Phoebe grimaced. "He was obsessed with controlling everything I did. I was just laughing with the stable manager about Sherry doing something funny. He went berserk."

"He wasn't right, and that's a problem here. There are not enough good men to go around."

"Have you met the new protectors?"

"We've seen them around. The girls talked to them, but they didn't react to them. So, they did a DNA scan for the mating project database."

"Blaze said there are about half a million cyborgs without mates. The AI will search the entire database for matches," I don't know what the odds are, but they will be lucky to get a match. The database includes offworld cyborgs, too."

"They are still young yet."

Once they get in the system, it won't take long at all to find a match if there is one," Phoebe assured her. "By the way, my garden is producing more than I expected. Can I bring you some vegetables when we come?"

"That would be wonderful, but how much can you carry on that sky cycle of Ranger Blaze's?"

"Enough for a few days. I can put in for a drone pick up to bring you some after that. How is your garden doing?"

"I planted late, but it's going to start producing in a couple weeks, I think."

"I will definitely schedule a drone pickup, and I will bring you some produce."

The two women chatted a little longer about Sara's girls and her worries about keeping everyone fed. Phoebe shared how Sara could use her comm-tablet to look for opportunities and information about the Enclave's assistance to help town dwellers make a living.

After Phoebe talked to Sara, she sat with Blaze on the loveseat sofa in their temporary quarters with his comm-tablet to look at housing that would be transported to their site in sections for assembly.

Their new dwelling would consist of a cluster of domes made from aerated concrete sections fused together onsite. A large dome would be centered in a small cluster of smaller domes. The center one housed the kitchen, dining and living area and lav. The smaller domes would be bedrooms with private bathrooms, sitting areas and storage for clothes and personal belongings. Their master bedroom would have all that plus and an attached nursery. They chose three peripheral domes to start with plans to add domes as they had more children.

Blaze also ordered the components of the security system he planned to install before returning to work.

The next day was Friday, when he'd originally planned to be home to take delivery of his new horse. The hover transport delivered his horse in the morning barely an hour after sunrise. Arthur was a classic chestnut gelding with white feathering around his legs.

"Oh Blaze, he's beautiful!" Phoebe exclaimed as the handler led him down the ramp into the pasture. "He's huge!"

Blaze was 6'6" and able to see over the horse's withers. The handler gave him the lead rope and returned to the transport to unload the horse feed.

"He is certainly an impressive animal," Blaze said, stroking the horse's neck. "Remember me, Arthur?" He had spent a few hours with the horse while deciding if the animal was for him.

The horse sniffed him and nickered as Blaze kept stroking him. After a few minutes of getting reacquainted, he walked Arthur around the pasture along the fence line. The field had been doubled in size soon after Blaze had closed the deal.

Bonding with an animal wasn't entirely a new experience for Blaze. Understanding Phoebe's attachment to her animals, he had made an effort to relate to them.

Phoebe was right; Arthur was a robust and fine-looking animal. The cyborg had downloaded a complete guide, including a video on training, riding, and maintaining horses. This was his first animal, and he wanted to make sure he met its needs properly.

Phoebe stood back with her horse Sherry watching Blaze interact with his horse. She couldn't help smiling as she watched him murmuring to the animal as they walked, holding the lead close to the horse's head. Arthur seemed to be paying attention, and Blaze looked happy with his new friend.

They had temporarily divided the pasture with a fence between two parts to give the two horses a chance to get acquainted before pasturing them together. The tiny goats had their own smaller pasture, so they didn't accidentally get trampled.

When he came around to the end of the pasture where Phoebe stood with her bay Sherry, he stopped a few feet away so the horses could get a look at each other. Sherry pricked her ears forward and looked up at Arthur with interest. He stretched his neck and sniffed.

Blaze advanced, but Sherry nipped at Arthur, who retreated before she could latch onto him. Arthur snorted indignantly. Phoebe and Blaze both laughed.

"She seems to be telling him she is the female in charge," said Blaze

"I thought she might like the company of another horse," Phoebe said with a slight frown. She looked up at her horse, and she was staring at Arthur with her ears pricked forward. "Well, she looks like she does."

Arthur nickered but kept his distance. "I think we can just let them get acquainted at a distance. He's smart enough to stay out of her way." Blaze unhooked the lead from the horse, wound it up, and took it to the new horse shed they'd built to house the two horses. He hung it on a hook inside then joined Phoebe to feed the rest of the animals.

When they finished, Blaze scooped her up in his arms and carried her into the house. "But I was going to pick some vegetables for dinner…"

"It's not dinner time yet," Blaze said innocently and gave her a longing look. "I need you now."

Phoebe looked up at him with an indulgent smile. On a normal day, they would still be in bed indulging their lust for each other. "Now that you mention it. I need some personal attention myself."

Instead of carrying her to the bed, he took her into the bathroom for a shower. Phoebe was hot and sweaty because she couldn't regulate her body temperature like Blaze could. While he enjoyed fucking her in the shower, it was incredibly crowded. Blaze had to crouch so his head wouldn't touch the ceiling and block the water.

He set her on her feet in front of the shower and pulled off his t-shirt over his head. When they were both naked, Blaze guided her into the shower stall and stood outside, leaving the door opened.

He grabbed the soap, turning it over and over in his hands until he accumulated ample suds to wash Phoebe. He commanded the unit to change to the mist setting and began to rub soap on her breasts first. She let him have free rein because she loved him, and because the experience was always incredibly pleasurable.

Phoebe raised her arms so he could rub soap under them between kneading her breast and tweaking her nipples. Just to be thorough, he soaped her arms and the rest of her torso. Pausing to make more suds, Blaze hunkered down to soap her legs from her feet to her pussy. Of course, he lingered at her pussy in between to wash all her folds.

Pulling down an auxiliary hose, he rinsed the soap away. Next, he wetted and washed the hair on her head and rinsed it thoroughly. Blaze then took his turn washing up in the shower, while Phoebe dried herself with a towel. She was about to detangle her long wet hair, when Blaze finished so she helped him dry.

He scooped her into his arms and carried her the few steps to the bed, laid her on it and climbed on after her. He started kissing her--- her forehead, her nose, her cheeks, then a long, slow, tongue tangling kiss.

He teased her slowly, dragging his mouth over her upper chest, kissing, licking, and nibbling, while skirting around her erect, aching nipples. When she started to caress his head, he took her wrists firmly but gently and pressed her hands open against the bed. He was letting her know he was in charge.

Phoebe smiled; she liked when he was in charge because she knew she could trust him to drive her wild with desire without hurting her… Well, maybe just a little, a pinch here, a nibble there…

She moaned as he took her nipple between his teeth and squeezed it to the edge of pain. Then he sucked on it while sliding a finger into her wet opening. Sliding a second finger inside, he pressed his thumb against her clit. He took the same care of her other nipple before working his way down her chest and belly. His hands on her inner thighs urged her to spread her legs wider, and then his mouth settled over her clit.

Phoebe keened as he alternately flicked his tongue over it and gently sucked. He stopped as her arousal was approaching orgasm to lap the juices from her slit. Then he stopped, leaving her on the brink. She crooned plaintively but remained poised as he'd placed her.

Blaze moved over her, took her face in his hands, and kissed her lips. He continued kissing her, and she put her arms around him. With her legs spread wide, he drove his cock into the hilt, holding her there.

It took him only a few hard thrusts to bring her to climax. Hugging him, she caressed him between the pleasurable contractions of her climax. He took her slowly while it played out, pausing to kiss her as she waned. She kissed him back, caressing him, and murmuring love words while he basked in her praise.

"I know what you want… What you need," she whispered. "I'm ready, my love."

In the months they had been together Blaze had shown his love in so many ways. Their lovemaking took them to an alternate universe where only they existed. Knowing what Blaze went through in the grueling ninety years of war he and his brethren fought for Earth, Phoebe wanted him to feel as much pleasure as he gave to her. She wanted him to feel loved as much as he loved her.

Blaze leaned back and smiled at her, his eyes sparkling with passion. "You will always be my favorite ride…" Kissing her, he pulled his cock most of the way out and slammed his hips against hers, thrusting into her. Soon, he was pounding into her, pleasuring her with his cock. Every stroke caressed her inner walls and her sweet spot in rapid succession careening them to the summit of ecstasy. Phoebe alternately mewled and huffed while clinging to his shoulders and pressing him to her.

The closer he drove her to rapture, the more she wailed and keened. She screamed his name with the onset, then aahed as he pounded through it and took her to another release and his own. Blaze roared as he pumped his essence into her. Phoebe came again.

Phoebe kissed and caressed him lovingly as their mutual orgasm shook them deeply. Blaze basked happily in her attention, nuzzling and kissing her back.

The terror of a few days ago receded into the back ground, driven back by their shared passion.

THIRTY

After their passionate interlude, they got cleaned up and went to get out fresh clothing to dress. They had just gotten a delivery of standard issue the day before to replace what they lost in the house.

But Blaze couldn't pass up the chance to take Phoebe again. Watching the sway of her hips as she padded naked toward built-in drawers, he strolled behind her and slid his hands over her breasts. He pulled her against him, so his hard length lay between her butt cheeks.

Phoebe smiled and leaned her head back against his chest, moaning a sigh. She could deny him nothing. Perhaps it was also because of the nights they spent alone craving each other that made them hypersexual when they were together. Whatever reason, she was usually receptive to his desires when they were together.

She didn't need much coaxing to crawl onto the end of their bed on her hands and knees, offering him her wet pussy for a quickie.

Phoebe's comm-tablet buzzed on the dining table twice before they finished. Neither of them was in any hurry to get to it. She thought it might be Sara or an answer to an information query she made. Nothing pressing that couldn't wait until she and her mate were sated.

When Phoebe picked up her tablet later, she found a vid message from Sara.

"Hi, Phoebe,

"Sorry to bother you. I-I know we planned for you to come on Monday, but I'd really appreciate it if you could come tomorrow instead. S-something's come up, and I really need to see you right away, and we could really use some goat cheese and eggs... T-there... There are a couple more mouths to feed... And supplies are running low. Let me know if you can make it tomorrow..."

Phoebe frowned and played it again.

"What's wrong?" asked Blaze, watching her.

"I don't know. Sara seems weird."

"We can go tomorrow, Phee, if you want."

"We never said anything about eggs and cheese, and she never stuttered before."

"She said there were more mouths to feed. We do have plenty of eggs and cheese."

"There's a new batch of chicks. Maybe I can ship some to her via drone. I can pick and pull some vegetables before dark, and we can leave first thing in the morning."

"I'll help you."

"That would be great, love."

Blaze glided the sky cycle in a circle around the block where Sara's house stood, scanning the area for anomalies. The Grafton protectors had reported few issues or problems since the Enclave representatives helped them set up a new town government.

Something was off, but he couldn't say why he thought it. Sara's body language when the vid-commed Phoebe made Blaze think she looked stressed. He didn't get anything suspicious on his internal scanner, yet the fine hairs in the back of his neck prickled just like they used to in the war just before the shooting started.

He decided in that split second; he should get Phoebe out of there. He heard a loud crack when he felt a sudden sting just below his right shoulder blade. Phoebe grunted and slumped against him. Then warm wetness spread on his back.

"Blaze!" Phoebe gasped.

He swung his leg over the front of the cycle and turned to catch Phoebe as she slumped forward before, she could fall onto the ground.

"Baby, no!" he cried, horrified. Blood oozed from the wound down the front of her shirt and over his arm in the back. Knowing she could die if he panicked, Blaze tamped down his emotions. The nearest medical center was in New Chicago, two hours away. That's why he always carried a medkit on his cycle.

The bullet had passed through her into his back and lodged against his rib. His nanites had already blocked pain from the damage. Soon, they would push the bullet out and close the remaining wound. But he knew Phoebe hadn't accumulated enough nanites from him to heal her wound.

Holding her with one arm, he opened the storage compartment behind the seat and pulled out the medkit. A small flyer lifted into the air down the street, pivoted, and shot off to the east.

Blaze knew it was probably the shooter, but his first concern was Phoebe. He'd let himself believe the danger was over after he took out Edmund Stone and rescued her.

The door to Sara's house opened.

"Oh gods, no!" Sara cried. "I am so sorry. Bring her in here."

While Blaze carried his mate into Sara's home, he had sent all the info on the flyer to the Grafton cyborg protectors. He took her into the kitchen and laid her on the kitchen table because she was still bleeding. Worse, she was having trouble breathing as the wound was sucking air into her chest.

The bullet had left a bloody hole over Phoebe's right breast. She was still bleeding and struggling to breathe. A quick scan told him the bullet had gone straight through her upper lung missing the major artery and heart. But it was too damn close.

Blaze opened the medkit and took out one of five syringes filled with nanites. He uncapped the tip, inserted it into the wound, and pushed the plunger, injecting the full bolus.

Once the nanites were injected, he covered the wound with a synthetic skin patch to stop more air from getting in while the nanites repaired the damage.

A second scan told him her wound was no worse than he thought. She was breathing a little easier.

"How is she, Ranger?" Sara asked meekly

"It's bad, but I think she'll make it. I've consulted our chief medic, and he agrees the nanites should heal her in a few days." Blaze pushed his fingers through his hair. "Do you want to tell me why you are sorry?"

"Clade Jeffreys Stone's second in command threatened to kill my daughters if I didn't get you here so he could get even for killing his half-brother. You killed Martin and took Phoebe, when he wanted her."

"I told him what Martin did to Phoebe and that she left on her own. I made the mistake of telling him that she was with you," Sara started to cry. "I didn't realize what he was going to do. His buddies were hurting Joanie, and he was going to let them 'break her in.'. I figured they were going to take turns raping her."

"He should have come for *me*!"

Sara sobbed. "He's as evil as his brother. He shot Phoebe to hurt you because he knows a cyborg loves his female above everything else." She cried harder. "I told him about the women Martin tortured and killed, and he didn't care. You took his brother, so he would take your mate."

"I shouldn't have killed him, but after Phoebe told me what he did to her and the other three, I became obsessed with making him pay. Had I ever dreamed someone would come after Phoebe... Twice. I might not have."

"I never knew Clade was his brother, too. Or anyone cared for him until Clade showed up half drunk on my doorstep with guns and two thugs," she said, sniffling. "That bastard Martin deserved everything he got."

Blaze was silent as he sat in a chair, holding Phoebe's hand in both of his as she lay unconscious on the table. His eyes welled with tears at the front of the khaki green t-shirt soaked with her blood. Seeing her like that was worse than any torture he had endured in the war.

Her pulse grew stronger, and she was breathing better, but she wasn't waking up.

"Kydel? It's been a half-hour, and she's still unconscious." Blaze reached out via the cyborg network.

"Have her vitals improved?"

"Yes, and the bleeding has stopped. Should I give her another bolus of nanites?"

"It won't hurt her if you do, and it could speed things up."

"Fuck, this is all my fault. I knew Cyborg Command wouldn't punish me for ending that serial killer. I never counted on him having relatives who might want revenge."

"Give me your coordinates, and I will send a shuttle down."

"Thank you, Kydel. I owe you."

THIRTY-ONE

Twenty minutes later, a shuttle from the *Starfire Nemesis* landed in the ancient street in front of Sara's house. Blaze strode from the house, carrying Phoebe, who lay limply in his arms. The door opened into a loading ramp, and he hurried inside, where he was surprised and relieved to see Kydel waiting with a stretcher.

"Thanks for coming, Kydel."

"Glad to help, brother."

As soon as Blaze laid her on the stretcher, Kydel put a tube into her arm to infuse nanite-laced intravenous fluids.

"I estimate she will wake by the time she finishes this bag," Kydel said. "We'll take her back to the ship, just in case of complications."

"I know my field medicine, but I was afraid of overlooking something important because I am terrified, I will lose her."

"It's good you were not so panicked that you didn't realize your weaknesses, which most of us hate to admit."

The shuttle lifted off as soon as Kydel had the IV set. Just as the Chief Medic had predicted, Phoebe had started to awake by the time they put her into a patient observation room.

"Oh Phoebe! Baby, I was scared out of my mind!" Blaze murmured, his eyes reflecting relief. He raised her hand to his lips and kissed it.

She drew in a breath and let it out. "I feel much better now."

"I am so sorry, Phee. Clade Jeffreys was Martin Stone's half-brother. He shot you to get even with me for what I did to Martin."

"I didn't know he was Martin's half-brother either."

"I shouldn't have killed Martin. That started this whole chain of events. But I *wanted* to kill him after you told me how he hurt you. My only regret is you got hurt twice more for what I did." *I enjoyed his pain... I enjoyed killing him...*

"Do you think you equated Stone the with the Mesaarkans who tortured you?" she asked barely above a whisper.

"I didn't think about it at the time. I kept visualizing him there beating you. Maybe once or twice I flashed back to my captivity, but what he did to you was foremost in my mind," he admitted. "But after Sara told me he was trying to woo you back to kill you too, I wasn't sorry. I am only sorry you suffered for it."

"You couldn't know, Blaze." Phoebe cupped her hand against his cheek. "He had to die. He wouldn't have let me go. He would have found a way to get to me and finish what he started."

"I think that might go for his half-brother as well…"

Blaze stopped speaking and seemed to stare into space for several seconds. "They got him."

"They got Clade?" Phoebe asked.

"Yes," Blaze said, visibly relieved. "They're taking him to New Chicago for transport to the prison planet. They have a vid of him shooting us."

"Us? Blaze are you, all right?"

"Fine. The nanites have already pushed the bullet out and closed the wound. One of my metal alloy ribs stopped it before it did any real damage."

Medic Kydel breezed into the room, looking from one to the other with a reassuring smile. "Now that you are awake and finished with the fluids, you can go to a crew cabin for the night. I don't foresee any other complications. You can shuttle back to Earth in the morning."

"Thank you, Kydel."

A short time later, a crewman from stores brought them new clothing to replace their blood-soaked garments. While Phoebe insisted that she could walk, Blaze carried her to their temporary cabin.

"I just want you in my arms," he told her and dropped a light kiss on her forehead.

She sighed and snuggled against him, resting her free hand on his shoulder. "I love you, too."

Inside the modest cabin, Blaze carried her to a small sofa and sat down with her on his lap. He just sat there, holding her with her head resting on his shoulder. A shudder went through his body.

"Blaze are you, all right?"

"I will be; that was just the most frightening thing that has ever happened to me." He shuddered again. "I was terrified you would die…"

Phoebe looked up at him, hearing the raw fear in his voice. She got up and turned, sitting back on his lap, straddling his legs and facing him. His midnight eyes shone with unshed tears. She put her hands on his cheeks and stroked them with her thumbs.

"But I didn't. I'm right here… Feeling better by the minute."

"I have never felt so weak and helpless in my life. I would rather face torture by the Mesaarkans again than lose you." Blaze looked angry as he admitted the last.

"Believe me sweetheart, I know exactly what you mean. We are each other's greatest weakness. I would rather face almost anything but the rest of my life without you. I never knew it was possible to love anyone this much."

"It's even worse than that. It's my fault he came to kill you because I killed Martin."

"Blaze, you didn't know. None of us knew he had any relatives. Martin deserved what he got."

"But you didn't."

"Neither did the other women he killed." She held his gaze while caressing him. "Blaze, I'm feeling fine now after all the nanites you pumped into me. It doesn't hurt a bit."

She started planting little kisses on his face all around his mouth but not on his lips, teasing him. He only took that for a few seconds before he held her head between his hands and pressed his lips to hers.

Blaze forgot everything but how she felt, warm and alive in his arms, kissing him back. He savored her lips on his, the taste of her as their tongues did a sensual dance. He put all his love for her in that kiss and felt it returned in her response.

They both became aroused early in the sweet, slow kiss with her body tight to his and her mons pressed against his hard cock.

But Blaze wouldn't take it any further. Phoebe needed more time to recover with the nanites sapping her body's resources to repair the damage. When they ended the kiss, Phoebe laid her head on Blaze's should her, and they just held each other. Minutes later, she drifted to sleep, and Blaze carried her to the bed. He put her on the bed and lay down beside her, watching her sleep.

She was going to be all right, and he would be, too.

By morning Phoebe was feeling fine, other than being ravenous. A full-body scan in the medical bay confirmed her recovery was complete. Three and a half hours later, they were back on Earth in Grafton, picking up Blaze's sky cycle.

As soon as the shuttle landed in front of Sara's house, Sara and her two daughters came out to greet them.

"Omigod! You gave us such a scare," Sara mused as she hugged Phoebe. "We cleaned the blood off the seat, and the protectors came and closed it up for you."

"Did they give you the food we brought?" Phoebe asked.

"Yes, thank you so much. We're going to be harvesting our own soon, though we won't be here much longer. Joanie just got matched to one of those protectors in Sun Valley, so we are moving there."

"Good for you!" Phoebe exclaimed. "After everything that's happened, you probably need to get away from this town. Let us know when you get settled, so we can come to see you."

"I will."

"Congratulations, Joanie. I think you will be very happy. I sure love this guy here." She went back to Blaze, slipping her hand in his. As she looked up at him, she surmised he was anxious to go home. "We have to get back."

The homestead was as they left it. The horses came to the fence near the house when the sky cycle settled down, reminding them that morning chores were a few hours late. Blaze fed the animals while Phoebe milked the goat. Only the nanny from her homestead had milk as the newer goats were still adolescents and never bred.

Next, Phoebe collected the eggs from the chicken coop. The hens from the chicks her last chicken hatched were laying eggs by then, so the number of eggs was significant. She had just started having a drone come once a week to take them out for trading.

When she finished with the goats and chickens, she found Blaze brushing out his new horse while talking to him. He was wearing the old battered Australian bush hat that he'd worn off duty during the war. He'd been wearing it the day they met. She was relieved to see him unwinding from the stress of the day before. Seeing that he was only about half finished, Phoebe decided to get out her brush for Sherry and groom her own horse as well. She found herself smiling as she drew the curry comb over her horse, that Blaze seemed so taken with Arthur.

That and the repetitive motions of grooming the horse were calming him. Phoebe thought they had worked out the trauma Blaze had suffered seeing her so grievously injured, but he had said little since they woke up on the ship. The haunted look she had seen in his eyes after she began to recover was back.

THIRTY-TWO

When they finished the chores, they were hot and sweaty, so Phoebe headed straight for the shower, making sure Blaze followed her. She started peeling off her clothes as soon as they were inside the bathroom. She had wanted Blaze when she woke early that morning on the ship, but he had not been up for it. He seemed almost afraid to hold her too tightly.

But the wound was gone entirely, without even a scar.

Phoebe made sure he was watching as she took off each piece of clothing. She knew he could scent her desire from the wetness between her thighs. When she was naked, she put her hands behind her head, fluffing her hair, and arching her back to draw attention to her breasts. Her nipples were hard and erect, and so was Blaze's cock.

He looked torn as she met his gaze. "Blaze, I am fine," she soothed and pointed to the spot where the wound had been. "See, it's all gone."

She stepped closer to him, deliberately brushing her nipples against his ribcage. He sucked in his breath with a hiss. She put her arms around his waist and pressed against him, kissing the middle of his chest. Then she raised herself on her toes to press her mons against the length of his erection.

As she lowered herself, her wet slit caressed his cock with the promise of bliss, and she closed her mouth over his male nipple, laving and sucking it. Phoebe backed him into the shower then went to work on his other nipple.

If he were trying to control his responses, it didn't work. He couldn't suppress a groan as Phoebe started kissing and nibbling her way downward. She gave the command for the mist setting as she knelt in front of him and started laving his cock. Gently fondling his scrotum with one hand, she took the head into her mouth, licking and sucking, working the rest with her other hand.

Her head bobbed forward and back as she took him as deep as she could. Blaze stroked her head, letting her have her way as he leaned against the shower wall. Phoebe could tell by the way his body tensed that he was close to orgasm. Seconds later he pulled back and his cum squirted over her upper chest and breasts.

Phoebe smiled up at him and laughed at the look on his face. He helped her up and called for the shower to rinse her off, then pulled her into his arms to kiss her. It was the kind of kiss that set her whole body on fire for him. They washed and dried and moved to the bed so Blaze could finish what she started. They made love until they were both spent.

"I'm getting two more rangers for Texas," Blaze said as they lay cuddled in bed afterward. "As much time as I've spent away, progress is slow. Many towns are run by honest people, and they don't need my services to get rid of tyrants and their gangs. Once we determine that, we can send in the protectors and municipal advisers to help them restore infrastructure."

"Does that mean your schedule is going to change?" Phoebe asked, stroking his chest.

"Yes, I will only be out three days a week."

"Mm, good. I think we can work with that." She leaned over to kiss his cheek, and he turned his head, so she kissed him on the lips instead. "Do you feel better now?"

He pulled her onto him, flattening her breasts against his chest and pressing his length against her clit. "Mm, yes. Much better."

Blaze and Phoebe spent the next week occupied with all the details of building their new home, securing their homestead, and caring for the animals and food crops. There were daily deliveries of modular components for the house, replacement furnishings and the multifunction security system.

The wreckage of the cabin was cleared away and they built the new home so the center of the largest dome was a few meters west of the cabin site. Nothing was salvaged from the original structure. Their new home included a modern version of a cook stove, as well as a food processor.

A two-man cyborg team with four androids put up the house in four days. A second team installed security cameras with scanners on every side of the property and a set of defense drones with anti-aircraft guns. All of it was integrated through their home AI. Blaze upgraded his onboard CPU so he could monitor it out in the field on the job.

The construction team was removing the temporary shelter as Blaze and Phoebe walked around inspecting their new home after chores.

"I still want you to have a cyborg bodyguard while I am away," Blaze said when the security system was completed.

"Okay."

"No argument?"

She thought he looked pleased. "No, argument. I saw how upset you were after the kidnapping and when we got shot. I don't want you to worry." They had added a guest house to their original plan with a separate entrance for the body guard.

"There could be other towns and villages infiltrated by officials with Eastern Overlord ties. Just because the Enclave has a treaty with them, doesn't mean they are abiding by it."

"Did they find out who leaked our location?"

"It originated in New Chicago. They could trace it to a stolen comm," he said. "That tells us the Eastern Overlords have plants inside the Enclave, and communications outside the cyborg network aren't secure."

"What are they going to do?"

278

"Secure the border something like I've done here. But mainly for flyers and hovercraft. We want to know who is coming into our territory and from where."

"With all the cyborgs and all the tech, can't you go in and shut down the Eastern Overlords?"

"The Federation won't let us. Somebody high up is protecting them. They have been since the war ended," Blaze explained. "Our treaty says they can't come into our territory without clearance. So far, that hasn't stopped them. We must enforce it."

"That reminds me, when do I get my new weapons to replace the guns I lost in the attack?"

"Delivered yesterday. They are in the house. I got you an ion rifle and a blaster. Before I go back on duty, I will teach you how to operate and maintain them."

"I hope I won't need them," she said.

"As do I." Blaze stopped and turned to face her, taking her into his arms. "Would you like to go inside and try out our new shower...?"

"Or the tub?"

Blaze smiled down at her and kissed lightly. "If you prefer…"

"Then there is that gorgeous new bed…"

"Mm."

"And I can feel that you are ready." Phoebe smiled and playfully rubbed the bulge in his pants with her hand.

"And you are going to get it, too" He scooped her up, cradling her in his arms and carried her into the house.

EPILOGUE

A week later, Blaze and Phoebe rode their horses together for the first time on the paths that Javen had cut through the property. Until he sat on his horse for the first time, he didn't truly understand Phoebe's affinity for them. He found it a relaxing way to enjoy the property surrounding their homestead. Blaze liked it especially because he and Phoebe did it together.

Phoebe was stronger now because of all the nanocybots she'd received for her injuries. Their mating was more satisfying than ever, and they had a plan to start their family in a few more months. Blaze was looking forward to seeing her belly grow round with their child.

He went back to work two weeks later feeling confident that Phoebe was safe at their new home. It was also rumored that word got around to the Eastern Overlords how his team went onto Edmond Stone's estate and took back his mate. Hopefully, that might discourage future incursions into Enclave territory.

Six months later, they were riding the trails when Phoebe pulled her horse up beside his on their favorite rise to look at the open country around them. Blaze was still wearing the battered old Aussie bush hat to shade his eyes. He could tell there was something different about her. Her scent was different, so he scanned her more than once, hardly daring to believe what he discovered. He didn't tell her though, because it was her place to tell him. At least that's what they told cyborgs in their virtual education.

Yet, he couldn't hide his broad smile when she looked up at him from beneath the brim of her similar bush had.

"You know, don't you?" Phoebe couldn't suppress her smile, either.

"You're pregnant."

"Yes. Isn't it wonderful?"

"It is, and I love you."

"I love you, too. And I have come to love this place, living here with you."

Blaze jumped off his horse and held his arms up for Phoebe to come down from her horse. He couldn't wait to hold her for a long slow kiss to celebrate the new life they created.

One thing led to another. There were two reasons they like that rise, the view and the tall oak shading it. It was a sheltered place for Phoebe to hold for a quick fuck. Phoebe laughed joyfully as Blaze moved them to the tree and placed her hands against it and started unfastening her pants. Her hat fell off first and then his fell off as he took her and poured his essence into her. He adored the way they could come together with spontaneity, and how open she was in her love for him. Having her in his life was so much more than he ever dreamed in the endless years he fought the war.

Blaze had finally found home in her and this place they both loved.

He would do his best to make it a fine place to raise children with the only woman he would ever love.

The End

.

Thank you for reading Blaze, Cyborg Ranger. I hope you enjoyed it and will leave a review here: http://amzon.me/blaze.

Find all my books at:
https://amazon.com/author/clarissalake

Keep in touch:

Visit my website at and sign up for my newsletter.

Everyone who signs up will get a free book.

Clarissa Lake's Other Works:

Szeqart Prison Planet Series
Soliv Four

Narovian Mates Series
Dream Alien
Alien Alliances
Her Alien Captain
Her Alien Trader

Farseek Mercenary Series
Commander's Mate
Lieutenant's Mate
Sahvin's Mate
Argen's Mate
Faigon's Mate

Farseek Warrior Series
Kragyn
Narzek

Roran

Wicked Ways

Interstellar Matchmaking
Korjh's Bride
Rader's Bride
Joven's Bride

with Christine Myers
Jolt Somber
Talia's Cyborg
Axel Rex
Dagger Jack

Website:
http://clarissalake.authors.zone/

Visit my website at and sign up for my newsletter.

Everyone who signs up will get a free ebook.